Save the Best for Last

Kim Hanks

Raider Publishing International

New York   London

First Printing

The characters in this book have no existence outside the imagination of the author, and have no relation whatsoever to anyone bearing the same name or names. They are not even distantly inspired by any individual known or unknown to the author, and all the incidents are pure inventions.

ISBN: 1-935383-09-4

Published By Raider Publishing International

www.RaiderPublishing.com

New York   London

Printed in the United States of America and the United Kingdom

By Lightning Source Ltd.

Save the Best for Last

Kim Hanks

CHAPTER ONE

At sunset on this very warm evening in April, Ms Darien said a quick good bye to her workmates and set off for home to find her family. It had been less than a month since she had started working for the Taji Corporation and she was in a hurry because she had promised Whitney Barnes a story about how difficult it had been to survive in the town of Green Oasis in the periods of the evil family and the church of darkness.

It was believed that the owner of this church had some evil powers that he acquired from the bangle from the bed of the ocean. These powers were so dangerous that, if any body who was not aligned to that church talked against it, he would immediately experience a problem in his life or could also die.

Most of the people in Green Oasis had stopped their children from telling each other stories about that family for fear of the immediate effects they felt in their lives. It was rumored that many followers of the church in Green Oasis had lost their lives as they had been offered as sacrifices.

However, after a long period of fear and distrust, the people organized a mob which demolished the church and killed two of its leaders. The younger son, Karl Hamilton, was however left alive due to the fact that, being very young, they believed he was innocent about his family's evil acts.

It was no wonder that as the family had been destroyed long ago, legends had grown up around it and so Ms Darien decided to tell her daughter the real story about that family that night.

She loved story telling and every night when she returned from work, she always had stories for her daughter.

But, on this particular night, on her way back home, within a few kilometers of the house, Ms Darien crashed her car into the wall.

She was not drunk, (she was, in fact, not in the habit of imbibing any type of alcohol), and her accident on the way back home elicited different opinions from different people. Judging by the way she veered into the wall most thought she had just lost control of the car. But others, a minority of the town elites believed they knew the real cause. They had seen such accidents happening in their town before. And although the church was no longer in existence, the 'accident' aroused a lot of suspicion in many people.

Beside the road was a brick wall, about 3 meters high from the raised ground. Some of the bricks had flown into the car, smashing all the glasses. Later, when the paramedics arrived on the scene, they found so much damage that, had they not known who it was they would never have identified Ms Darien as the victim. Though she was still in her seat with her head resting on the steering wheel, she was covered with bricks that flew into the car. The skin of her face had been peeled off and her cheekbones were shattered. Further, her whole face had been depressed into her forehead. She was fatally injured in the accident and was rushed to hospital. The paramedics feared she would die on the way to the hospital, but she made it there.

Considering her grievous injuries every friend and relative who visited Ms Darien in the hospital believed she would never recover from her accident, in spite of receiving the most intensive medical care in the town's most reputed and state of the art hospital.

For about six weeks after her accident, Ms Darien had not moved a bone nor a single muscle in her body as she lay on the bed, albeit technically alive. Her daughter and husband prayed hour after hour at her bedside.

Her friends who visited her regularly were sure they would one day have to say good-bye to her seeing how she was disabled, may never be capable of using her legs ever again and was in a constant coma.

Many, including her daughter, cried whenever they saw what had happened to her face, and what made it worse was that the local doctors could not guarantee that even surgery would return it to its previous appearance or erase the scars.

When, after spending a long two and a half months lying like a zombie in the hospital, she was finally declared fit to be taken back home, although there were some who one thought she might as well have been dead.

Not a day passed by when the doctors did not visit her at home where she lived with both her husband and her daughter Whitney Barnes. Not a day passed by when they did not try something new which they hoped would benefit Ms Darien in some way.

Whitney was at a loss whenever she wondered about what had really caused her mother's accident because she knew her mother was always very careful about every thing she did- and that included driving. No matter how much her father tried to comfort her and whether she was at their beautiful home in Green Oasis or on the university campus, she always appeared teary and upset.

One morning, Whitney woke up from her bed as she always did and readied herself for the day's lectures at university.

"Good morning, Dad? How is mom today?" Whitney asked her father.

"Morning, too, sweetheart. I'm afraid she's not very much better," Mr. Taji said.

One of the wealthiest and most easily recognized persons in Green Oasis, Mr. Taji Alistair, Whitney's father was still looking for the surgeon who he simply knew was out there and who he simply knew could treat his wife successfully.

Deeply affected by his wife's accident and remembering how robust and out going she had been in times gone by, he worried she may never return to her normal self. He could not bear the idea of her being incapacitated in any way.

Whitney, the apple of his eye, was his only child, his wife having been advised against any more pregnancies after a difficult delivery with Whitney. She had grown up confident in the love and care she received and assured by the comforts her family wealth afforded her. Now, a beautiful young lady, she was doing her bachelors degree in European Arts at Green Oasis University where she was adored by one and all.

In spite of her popularity, though, there was nothing Whitney valued more than spending time with her mother. This was a loving and devoted family and Whitney loved her mother passionately.

It was little wonder then, that through this trying period Whitney thought nothing of skipping lectures to look after her mother if the situation warranted it, which was quite often. As she watched her beloved mother on the bed, trying to communicate with her but not succeeding, Whitney's eyes would fill with tears.

But on this particular morning Whitney decided to attend the lectures at university, so she drove there in the brand new car her father had gifted her on her recently celebrated 19th birthday.

Mr. Taji was popular among the citizens of Green Oasis. Despite the fact that he was rich, as was also extremely helpful to anyone in distress. He employed over two thousand people from the town in his businesses.

There upon another morning.

Whitney arrived at the campus a little late and on entering the lecture room, found the hall already full. She started looking around to see where she could squeeze herself in, but was unable to locate a vacant seat.

"Hi. Would you like to sit here?" a young boy

asked Whitney, pointing to a little space near him into which he believed she could squeeze herself.

Whitney felt a flash of excitement. He was not really her friend but she accepted the seat all the same.

"Oh, nice, Thank you," Whitney said with little smile hovering about her lips.

As soon as the lectures were over, they all walked out of the class.

"What's your name?" Whitney inquired of the young man, emboldened by the fact that he had offered her with a seat.

"Oh, I'm Zwick Lamps and all my friends prefer calling me by that name," he replied.

"Sure. Nice to meet you. I'm Whitney Barnes," she said introducing herself.

Later, they moved out of the room together and went directly to the parking lot, engaged in light conversation.

"Can I give you a lift back home?" Whitney asked, and this was the beginning of their relationship.

"Wow! Thanks," he replied with a sound that wasn't a real laugh to his new friend, as he immediately he jumped into the car.

On the way to Zwick's home, there was an awkward silence for some time. Then Whitney asked him,

"Do you live with your parents?"

"Not really, I'm living with my uncle, a Mr. Dean Rogers. He is as good a parent as any I have ever seen, though. I had some problems when I was a kid, and my parents were unable to care for me so I ended up living with my uncle," he said pensively as he continued looking at her.

"Sorry, but my mom was in an accident and she hasn't recovered yet," Whitney explained while nodding her head in an apologetic way as by then she was unable to control her tears and they started rolling down her cheeks.

"Oh, was that the Taji case? I heard about that. It was so terrible," said Zwick, as he shook his head,

"Yes. Now she is totally disabled," said Whitney, her voice breaking as she scarcely breathed.

"I'm sorry," Zwick said gently and then continued, "As for myself, everyone thought it would be quite impossible for me to live up to this age because when I was young, both my parents were cursed by an evil family that lived here some time back. However, they managed to leave me at Madam Tabitha's place. She is a very wise old woman who can tell of the past and predict the future of this town. When I was there nobody ever came for me, until finally, 5 years later, my uncle came to pick me up. I was happy to meet my parents again, but they soon disappeared for good and no one has seen or heard from them since then," Zwick narrated as Whitney looked at him quite in wonder.

And then, Whitney asked awkwardly to confirm,

"Is that old lady still there now?"

"Yes," Zwick replied. She is still like my mother and treats me like her son. My own feelings toward her are really positive and I seek her advice before I take any important step." Zwick said, as if things were now better, but his voice was deeply sad.

"Does she have any children of her own?" Whitney asked him anxious to know more.

"No, Madam Tabitha, that is her name, said she was unlucky not to have children as the man she had to marry committed suicide on day of their wedding. After that big disappointment she decided to live on her own."

It was this first conversation that marked the beginning of Whitney's and Zwicks' friendship. They being classmates and both doing the same course would help to nurture it of course.

After dropping Zwick off at his home, Whitney sped on to hers, anxious to meet her mother soon, but when she reached home, she found her father already there.

"You were late today?" Mr. Taji asked Whitney as he plunked himself on the sofa.

"Yes dad." She looked at him. "I gave my new

friend a lift," she explained

After a light conversation of this and that Mr. Taji requested Whitney to stay with her mother, as he was going to the hospital where he had an appointment with the doctor.

Mr. Taji so loved his wife that he had given up his businesses in order to care for her and to find the best surgeons who could operate on her face which was still wrapped in bandages.

At times he and his daughter were upset at not being able to communicate with her since her accident.

"Dad, Mom wanted to say something the last time you had gone to the hospital but I could not understand her because she was so unclear," Whitney remarked to her father one day.

"Huh, what are you talking about?" Mr. Taji asked her.

"Yes, believe me, I saw her and I paid attention to her, but she just could not communicate," Whitney said.

"I'm gonna talk to the doctor about that when she goes in for a TV scan." Mr. Taji said, after considering her daughter's statement.

However, he was quite uncertain as to what Whitney was really trying to say to him.

Whitney went to the campus once more that day. Mr. Taji stayed at home waiting for the doctor.

For the most part Whitney lived a private life but now she had a new friend, Zwick. Zwick, too, was eager to create a very strong bond between them since they shared so much. At times Whitney could feel herself loosening up in spite of her mother's illness, and her new friend could sometimes make her forget what was happening at home for a short time at least.

Many students at university liked Whitney but she was not very good at making friends easily and besides, her family status, although making her famous enough in Green Oasis town, also made her wary of others. Her performance at University was quite good. She had once even participated in the junior Miss Green Oasis University contest which had made her quite famous on campus.

When the doctor arrived at the beautiful Taji home he found Whitney not yet back from the campus but Mr. Taji anxiously awaiting him. He immediately set about examining Ms Darien.

"How is she now?" Mr. Taji asked anxiously when he seemed to have finished.

"Well, she's still very weak but we need to perform the operation at the earliest because if we delay it for too long it could have serous repercussions," the doctor finally answered.

Mr. Taji expected so much from the operation that he had arranged for special surgeons from Germany to come and operate on his wife. Not wishing to distract Whitney from her studies, he tried to hide the true facts about his wife's condition from her.

CHAPTER TWO

In the next few days Zwick and his friend, Matt Fletcher attended a football training session because they were part of the university football team and a series of inter university football matches were coming up that semester. They therefore concentrated on keeping fit and preparing for the tournament. Green Oasis University would be having their opening matches soon. At the same time Whitney had not attended university for a whole week as her mother's conditions had suddenly taken a turn for the worse.

It was a Friday evening when the first match was played against Shepherd's University. But by the 90th minute, Green Oasis had taken the lead with 3:1 goals and the crowd went wild. However, Whitney was not present to join in the frenzy of the game. This time Zwick did not play as he spent all the time on the bench, but his friend Matt was in the starting line up and he contributed greatly to their glory.

Now Green Oasis University had qualified for the semifinals. And although Zwick did not play in the first game, he was not discouraged. Instead he continued training as he hoped to be sent on to the field one day soon.

"I didn't see your friend at the previous match but I hope she will make it for the coming one," said Matt as he and Zwick relaxed after a grueling workout.

"Yeah. She was sorry to miss the match too, but she wasn't able to leave her mother alone that day." replied Zwick, his arms swinging loosely.

"She has a sick mother? No you're kidding Zwick,"

Matt remarked awkwardly.

"Yeah. She was in an automobile accident and is now disabled. That's why you see Whitney very rarely on campus," Zwick announced in a very proprietary manner seeing that Whitney was now his close friend.

"Oh, that's bad," said Matt looking concerned although he wasn't really a friend of Whitney's yet.

That night, shortly after dinner, Zwick called Whitney to inform her about their victory over the other football team and to let her know that they had qualified for the semifinals. Although she had not watched the match, Whitney was happy for Zwick and the team. After wishing her a good night and as he readied for bed Zwick wondered whether it was Ms Darien's worsened condition that had Whitney missing school so much.

At around 10:00am the next morning, Zwick and Matt drove up to the paddock where Mr. Dean's horses were, and where Zwick was employed to do some housecleaning. It was while he was still painting the stable for the horses that he noticed a new watch gleam on Matt's hand.

"Where did you get that expensive watch?" Zwick asked Matt thoughtfully.

"I personally couldn't afford such a watch," Matt answered, but it's my friend Karl who gifted it to me. I'm sure you know that guy. He's famous on the campus because he's one of the richest students. If you remember he came to our first match driving a black Mercedes Benz."

Zwick woke up early the next day so that he could meet Matt on the campus before they moved to the pitch for the football match. But he found the lecturer already holding a class, and so he attended it. From there, many students went directly to the pitch. Zwick and Matt were scheduled for another game that day. After their preparations and a little briefing, the two decided to arrive earlier before the team line up. Meanwhile on their way, Zwick telephoned Whitney to ask whether she was coming this time. But unfortunately he did not get her on line.

14

However, he knew she always wished him success.

"We missed her again," Matt said grinning while Zwick nodded disappointedly.

By the time they reached the stadium, students for both Noel's academy and Green Oasis University were already in the pavilion cheering on their teams. Unfortunately Zwick, who desperately wished to make his debut on the campus team, would have to sit this match out too. Matt was selected for the first line up.

The match began and Green Oasis played quite well in the first few minutes after kick off. Their chancellor had promised them a party if they won which must have motivated them. Unfortunately a short time later Noel's academy was leading with one goal and the first half ended with Green Oasis not having scored at all.

Back in action, after the interval the determined Green Oasis team scored their first goal in the last minute of the second half. It was scored by Kent Larsson who had been assisted by Matt. Unfortunately, Matt was injured as they were going for the extra time crash, and so the coach ordered Zwick to warm up so that he could fill in for Matt.

Thirty minutes later, Green Oasis University supporters were celebrating their team's qualifying in the finals after beating Noel's Academy in the extra time goals at 4-1. Not surprisingly, this match increased Zwicks' popularity at the campus. No student who had watched him go on to the field ever expected he would score the fantastic goals he did against Noel's Academy with unstoppable dribbles. Now they would never forget it.

"Zwick you must be having a magic secret, man, the way you played in this game," Matt whispered happily to Zwick.

"Why do you say that? That isn't good talking," Zwick responded politely.

"No, it just surprised me that during the training you were never as superb as you wee today. You were so speedy and tough at dribbling," Matt said as he continued smiling

Secretly Matt thought Zwick must have some secret to it, despite the fact that he had displayed his unique abilities. It had been a surprise to all as they have never seen the guy play like that before.

"It's just luck and a lot of hard work that helped me do so well today. Who knows? I may not be so successful the next time." Zwick mused.

In the mean time, lectures continued as usual. One day, after their lectures Zwick took Matt and a new friend Kent to visit Whitney and her mother who was still unwell.

Mr. Taji welcomed them in as Whitney was busy in her mother's room.

"What a nice house this is, guys," Matt whispered to Zwick as the three of them settled down in the spacious living room.

Soon after, Whitney made her appearance. "Hi guys, have you all came to visit me? What a pleasure!" she remarked.

"Yeah, we have," they said.

"I'm... we're all...actually good, and... these are Matt and Kent. They are my friends," Zwick said as he tried to introduce his company to Whitney.

"Oh, nice to meet you too, guys." Whitney said, as she welcomed Kent and Matt as her new friends too.

Both Matt and Kent were stunned by Whitney's beauty. They chatted with her in a light-hearted manner as they helped themselves to the delicacies she served.

Later that night, after spending most of the day at Whitney's, Zwick returned home.

He flopped on to his bed and looked straight at the ceiling fan above him, watching the blades move in a slow rhythmic way. Abstractedly, he turned the head to the nearby table on which he had placed the necklace he always wore on his throat. Suddenly electrified, he noticed his necklace was glowing red. He stared at it for a moment and then lay back with a sigh taking it to be either a reflection of the light or a dream.

But later, after he switched off the light, he noticed

nothing had changed and the necklace was still glowing. Then it dawned on Zwick that he was not dreaming. Yes, Madam Tabitha had given him the necklace but she had not told him it had supernatural powers.

Feeling totally changed after he discovered his secret, he recollected how Matt and the other students had remarked on the extraordinary speed with which he had scored the three goals that helped defeat Noel's Academy. Filled with conflicting emotions, Zwick decided to put the necklace back on his neck and determined to keep this secret to himself.

Zwick woke up later than usual next morning and had to rush to meet up with his teammates preparing for the final match. On reaching the gym he found them more than halfway through their meeting. They were joined by Karl, another student who had inherited his late parents' wealth when they had died some years earlier. He had come to the meeting as he wanted to talk to his friends before they played the final match.

All the footballers listened to him as he egged them on with words of encouragement.

"But you will make it guys, just play as one!" he said.

"I bet we'll win, guys, come on," Zwick said with a smile after Karl had left.

In fact they all looked ready and determined to play. Zwick thought of his secret which he had determined not to share with anybody. Up to then nobody knew about it, including his close friend, Matt

This time Whitney was among the cheer leaders in the pavilion as the match between Green Oasis University and Rangers University began.

When the game started and Zwick started on the pitch, he was marked closely by his opponents who were acutely aware of his feat of scoring the three goals that knocked Noel's Academy out of the competition. Unfortunately, this did not save Rangers University. They

17

could not guess that Zwick had special powers to help him maintain his pace and dribble the ball such at a speed that they could not keep up with him, and by the time the final whistle blew Zwick had single handedly scored five goals against Rangers University. Zwick had single handedly helped Green Oasis University win the trophy and this made him name more popular on the campus.

Later, after the celebrations were over, studies went on as usual. Since the semester was about to end, the students were assigned after campus study groups in which they would have to conduct their discussions and complete their assignments. According to their selections, Whitney, Karl, Matt and Kent were all in the same group, while Zwick was grouped with Marie Parker, Rai Evans and Lisa Goodman. Zwick was not pleased with this as he had hoped to be with Whitney.

Matt, Kent and Karl were pleased with Whitney being in their group. Although Zwick was not, he tried to behave as if nothing was amiss. Later, when they were given assignments, Zwick did not really feel comfortable working with his group, but he tried to cope up with the situation since it was only for study purposes.

During the discussion when all the groups shared one room, his eyes kept constantly returning to Whitney. Then, when it seemed he was paying more attention to Whitney's discussion than his own group's, Rai raised her hand and broke Zwick' concentration on Whitney.

"Zwick are you here with us?" Rai asked.

"Umm. Repeat that question?" he said, after thinking for a minute, pretending to be following the discussion.

In fact, the more Zwick saw Kent, Matt, and Karl laughing and sharing within their study group, he began to imagine they were fooling around although they were actually right on track with their discussions.

As soon as the discussions were over, Lisa remained at the table with Zwick while Rai moved on. It was then that she advised him not to spend too much time with Rai as Karl would not like it. The rumors were that they were dating each other.

A short time later Zwick left the campus in Whitney's car. But this time, as they were on the way, Whitney remarked, "I had rarely seen Karl before the discussion groups."

"Yeah. He's quite a guy. Imagine owning your own business while still studying. And he was so supportive of our football team during the competitions," was the polite reply from Zwick.

"I've heard that his parents are dead?" Whitney enquired again after Karl who was turning into quite an enigma on the campus.

"Yeah, he was the young boy left when both of his parents were attacked by the people because of their evil ways. Both of them were torched for promoting the church of darkness. When Karl grew up, he inherited the property which had belonged to his parents," Zwick explained to her.

"Someone told me he is dating Rai, the blonde haired girl in my group. However, friends close to her told me that she is afraid of Karl's family background, so she doesn't seem to be really interested in him," he added.

After the long day at the campus, Whitney knew she had to tell her father about their new study groups and the many friends she had made on the campus. Talking to her father about the day's events always helped her to focus on other things besides her sick mother.

But no sooner had she reached home, and before she could even call a hello, she saw her father coming out from her mother's bedroom. Mr. Taji looked extremely sad and it was not difficult to see that he could not hold his tears back for much longer. Then he approached Whitney and hugged her.

"Whitney, Whitney! Your mom is...." Mr. Taji said in very sad tone looking straight into Whitney's eyes.

He cried as he failed to complete the statement to his daughter who was ignorant of what had happened to her mother.

Ms Darien had finally lost her lengthy battle with the injuries suffered in the accident.

"What's going on, Dad?" Whitney gasped as she saw her dad crying inconsolably.

"I'm sorry Whitney, the doctors did their best, but her blood pressure plunged to dangerously low levels, and they could do nothing". He explained already in deep mourning.

"She clung to life and it was a miracle she hung on for so long, but time ran out on her. She left before the surgeon could get here," the family physician commented.

This now was a turning point in Whitney's life. Stung by the shock of her mother's death she had only her father to turn to. Of all the misfortunes she had ever experienced surely this was the worst. She had accepted her mother being crippled and she would have accepted her even being as good as a vegetable, because she would at least still get to see her everyday, but she didn't feel she could ever get used to her dying when she did. She knew her mother's injuries had been serious but if the distance between Germany and Green Oasis had been shorter perhaps her mother might still have lived.

The burial service took place the following day. Stunned and still unable to come to grips with her loss, Whitney could not murmur even a single word. Looking across to the other side of the cemetery, she did notice, though, that her fellow students had come to attend the funeral. And they did look smart in their uniforms.

With Zwick taking the lead, the friends came over to Whitney and tried to comfort her in her time of grief. Their support meant a lot to Whitney and she was glad for their company during and after the service. Zwick especially seemed most attentive.

Whitney tossed and turned that night, unable to get the memory of her mother out of her mind. It was only when dawn crept in that she finally drifted off into a restless sleep.

Her mother's death affected Whitney for quite some time as she tried to adapt to life with only her father. Her friends Zwick and Kent kept her amused as well as they could and helped her overcome some of the pain, at least temporarily.

A month passed and Whitney had not yet resumed attending university. However Zwick proved himself to be a friend indeed. He was constantly by her side and never left her alone for as long as he could help it.

Finally, the group studies were over. Whitney, as was now usual, had not come to join in the discussion.

Karl took Zwick aside and told him that he and the other friends in the group had organized a small party for Whitney, in the hopes of bringing some normalcy back into her life. It was to be a surprise.

Since Karl was the only one in the group that had a steady income he decided to face all the costs of the party which would involve traveling to the resort at Dead Sea Beach.

Everyone was very excited about it except for Zwick. He had a different opinion. He did not insist due to the fact that he could not decide for Whitney, although he thought she still needed more time before she started partying again. But because he was in the minority, he promised to talk to Whitney about it. And sure enough, Whitney agreed to the plan due to the fact that all her friends were also going except for Rai who claimed she was not well enough for a journey to the Dead Sea. However, she wished them luck.

The Dead Sea Resort was quite far from Green Oasis. This beach was a popular spot for teenagers because of its perfect location and the therapeutic powers of the water. However the main objective was to entertain Whitney and distract her from the memories of her mother who had just passed away that previous month. As there were quite a good number of people at the party, Zwick stood aside with Whitney.

"But why did this guy do all this for me?" Whitney

asked Zwick about Karl after thinking about it quietly for some time.

But before he could reply, Karl interrupted.

"Whitney, have fun!" he said as he came up to them while they were enjoying the serenity of the beach.

Whitney and Zwick started moving about the beach glancing at their friends who were having fun. As they did so, Karl his pals started diving deep into the sea, but Zwick and Whitney continued strolling on the sands. After a while Karl was seen diving even deeper into the waters until he touched sand and was at the bottom. As he moved closer to the sea creatures he noticed something glittering on the sea bed. Realizing that it was a real bangle, he immediately picked it up and took it with him back to the surface. Surprisingly, he did not tell any of his friends he had come with, about his discovery in the sea.

A day later, the others were still talking about their wonderful experience at the resort. Whitney was tired as she was not used to this type of activity. As for Rai, her friends began to realize that she had not gone with them in order to avoid Karl who was trying to date her and had instead claimed that she was not feeling well. This had not stopped Karl from going ahead with the trip.

Late that same evening, Karl stayed home waiting for Rai as he had invited her to his home once they were back from the Dead Sea. Rai, however, had decided not to visit him. This was a big disappointment to Karl who had waited all day for this time with her.

The next day Karl went to the campus expressly to meet Rai and find out why she had disappointed him. He found Rai reading her material under a palm tree.

"Rai, how dare you disappoint me like that?" Karl asked Rai rudely.

"You know, I just had too much work and time was against me so there was no way I could make it," she retorted mockingly as she continued reading her material and swinging her legs.

In a huff, Karl decided to quit talking to Rai and

moved on.

It was at this very time that Marie dashed through the door of their lecture room.

"What happened between you and Karl? I saw you two quarreling. What is it?" Marie asked Rai.

"Nothing much, but he is angry with me because I failed to meet his demands. I don't love him and I'm not that kind of fool to be toyed with by him," Rai replied, determined to squash all rumors that she was dating Karl once and for all.

"Tell me, are you serious?" Marie asked wonderingly.

"Yeah, I don't care who he is. I was thoroughly disgusted when I learned about his family back ground.

After their assignments were handed in, the students continued with lectures and study group discussions.

Then, Zwick decided to meet Rai and Marie to complete the assignment before they left the campus as Whitney's group had also done that day. In fact, a deep acrimony had developed between Rai and Karl and Rai did not wish to talk to Karl as she confessed to Marie in the hostel.

CHAPTER THREE

Come Monday and the students were back at university in their lecture hall. As they waited for the lecturer, Zwick and Whitney sat in the second row content in each other's company. They had not met that weekend but Whitney had had no trouble finding Zwick on the campus on Monday. Regardless of Whitney narrating how life was difficult for her when she was alone, Zwick started imagining what a precious couple they would make once he fell in love with Whitney and she with him. Zwick knew the day would soon come when he would be in love with her. Whitney was not a bad choice, Zwick felt. He always choked up whenever he thought of telling her what was on his mind and in his heart. He really had strong feelings for her but he had problems expressing himself easily.

Whitney's amazing beauty kept Zwick enthralled whether she was in or out of sight. then, one day, an opportunity presented itself and it looked as though Zwick would no longer be able to avoid it.

"But, Zwick, why is it that your mind is always wandering?" Whitney asked him mischievously one day, as she saw him daydreaming distractedly as usual.

Zwick pretended to be busy to avoid answering her and lowered his eyes with embarrassment. He let the opportunity once more slip him by.

When the lectures were done, and they were both leaving the room, Whitney asked Zwick whether he had a problem.

"No, I'm….. just worried about my uncle; he's not in town at present," Zwick replied, trying to dodge the issue, despite the fact that it was his admiration for Whitney that was making him uncomfortable and not permitting him to tell her the truth.

The next day, Zwick had to go to the paddock where the horses were grazing. Although he had an appointment with Matt, this did not stop him from going to the farm first. It was while he was busy with his work that his mobile phone rang.

"Hello? Oh, hi, Whitney. Yes, I've missed university today. I'm busy at the farm," Zwick could hardly speak in his excitement.

"Ok, I'll be there soon, just wait for me," said Whitney.

Zwick carried on with his chores, anxiously waiting for Whitney, although he half believed she wouldn't really come.

But she did.

"Ha, ha, ha, Woo, it's quite amazing. In fact I thought you were kidding about this," Zwick said and waited for a moment.

"Oh, it was a promise, really, but I've just came to inform you that the test we were to have tomorrow has been postponed for next week. Now we have a full week to master the material," she said with her lovely smile.

"Are you serious? That's good news. I sure wasn't prepared for it." Zwick replied, surprised, as he carried on with his work. "Now we'll have enough time to prepare for it."

"This horse looks so healthy, you know," said Whitney. "It's so attractive," she said stroking the horse and beaming happily at it.

"Can you ride? Zwick asked her.

"No, I have never tried it but I will not fail to if ever I get the chance to try."

It was then that Zwick decided to teach her all about riding horses. The first time round was easy enough as Zwick rode alongside her on another horse. But soon she developed enough confidence until finally she made it alone. Zwick had proven to be a good instructor and by the time the training was over he was pleased that Whitney was now capable of riding a horse.

It was also a sizzling moment for Whitney because she had never thought of acquiring horsemanship skills. This event deepened their relationship.

That night, as Zwick lay on his bed, in spite of his previous attempts at trying to ignore his burning desire for Whitney, he now realized that he had really taken a fancy to her after their time on the farm.

Unfortunately, Whitney was ignorant about all that was going on with Zwick because he never said anything to her.

"Well, as a matter of fact, she is my best friend and very nice," Zwick muttered to himself confusedly. He groaned, as he realized how crazy he was for the beautiful Whitney who herself showed no signs of recognizing this.

"She is so cute and smart," he said to himself over and over again.

Later that night he decided to phone Matt so that he tell him about all that had happened at the farm.

CHAPTER FOUR

As time passed, Whitney finally gradually grew accustomed to life without her mother and continued with her studies at Green Oasis University.

One afternoon, Zwick was moving through the compound when he met Kent and they moved on together towards the lecture room.

"Where is Whitney?" Kent asked brightly

"She's visiting her grand mother in town with her father, today, so I don't think she will make her appearance here," said Zwick.

"I guess you must be missing her," Kent said and laughed at Zwick.

"Of course, isn't she our friend? I must feel concerned when she is not here," Zwick argued, managing to hide his real feelings.

Previously, Kent was convinced that Zwick was in love with Whitney, but now he wondered whether they really were just good friends. On learning that Whitney was not actually dating Zwick, he tried to see more of her. Being in the same study group with Whitney, he persistently stared at her with a look of adoration in his eyes although he was friendly enough to all the group members.

Although a secret admirer of Whitney, Zwick was not yet ready to openly express his feelings for her, half fearing that Whitney would respond negatively after having been friends for so long. That evening, before they left the campus, Zwicks' group was adjudged top place among the study groups. Rai and Marie, meanwhile, scored the highest marks in Zwicks' group.

After their good performance in the group activities, Marie and Rai were offered an opportunity by the Chancellor to publish the university news paper.

Marie couldn't wait to break the good news to Rai.

"Rai, Rai, I have wonderful news," Marie shouted out.

"Hmm, what is it?" Rai asked Marie, looking at her enquiringly.

"We have been appointed to publish the university's new paper," Marie said excitedly

"What?" she asked and continued, "But considering what?"

"We performed well, with highest marks in the group test we did recently," Marie explained.

This was wonderful news for both of them. Rai's secret ambition was to be a journalist one day and this was a godsend for the two of them, neither of whom slept a wink that night. However, early in the morning they were at the office that was assigned to them and from where they would conduct their duties.

As Rai went through her emails, she was surprised to find a note from Karl. She glanced at it and noticed that he was apologizing to her for the last incident that had led to some serious acrimony between them. Rai was quite surprised to receive this email as she had thought that by now everything would be over between them, which was why she decided not to show the message to Marie. So she sat down in their new office and read the article that Marie had written on their tour that Karl had organized to the Dead Sea.

And after reading it she remarked, "I think now he will be happy with Whitney, if he succeeds."

"What do you mean?" Marie asked.

"I know there must be other intentions behind Karl organizing that party for Whitney, and you know how guys behave, Marie. And this was a very expensive party, even though he is rich. It must have been a special one."

Meanwhile, Karl, who lived alone in the old chateau that had belonged to his late parents, had just got out of the shower. He sat down on a sofa and leafed through the album of photographs of them at the Dead Sea resort. He then stared through the window, and watched the sun set.

Going back to the album, he stared closely at Rai's face in a photograph. Finishing with her, he turned to Whitney looking at the photo with a very keen eye.

"She is really, stunningly charming," Karl said to himself as he poured a drink.

It took him a few seconds to finish it and moments later he picked up the jacket he had taken with him on the trip to the Dead Sea. Within a few seconds, he took out the golden bangle from the pocket. Interested, he decided to wear it, and began to imagine what a lovely gift it would make for Whitney. But then he noticed something mysterious. Suddenly before he could remove it, his arms started shivering and his eyes clouded over and turned black. Try as he might he found himself incapable of removing it from his arm.

In a while he started screaming in a high pitched voice until he heard a strange voice loudly saying, "We have come to save you."

At the same time, the weather outside had suddenly changed. There was a strong spinning maelstrom of wind, and thunder storms swept through the town of Green Oasis.

Then, it stopped as suddenly as it had started and Karl found himself lying on the floor in his sitting room. Coming back to his normal self he tried to open his eyes. Unfortunately he was not able to recall all that had happened to him. Then, he stood up and checked himself in the mirror. He was surprised to find he had not even a scratch on him although he realized the bangle was missing from his wrist.

Looking around the room, he could only see thin little particles of shining gold around where he had been lying and this puzzled him all the more as he failed to recall what had happened to him. Then he lay back and fell into a deep sleep.

The next morning, Karl woke up feeling extremely weak and drained of all energy. Later he switched on the radio. All the channels were airing news bulletins of the spinning maelstrom winds measuring 380 knots per hour, and thunder storms that had destroyed so much property in the town. The Green Oasis metrological station had had not even the slightest inkling of the impending disaster.

Going to the window Karl noticed a large dent in the compound wall and some trees that had been uprooted. But despite all the strange occurrences the disappearance of the bangle mystified him the most.

On his way to the university Karl couldn't help but notice the destruction everywhere. It was the same story when he reached the campus. Every student had a different opinion about what had caused this disaster which was unlike anything they had seen in decades.

Zwick and Whitney sat earnestly talking at a table where Kent soon joined them.

"The wind was so strong that it almost blew my roof off," Kent was saying half in jest, which made everybody grin.

Their attention was then drawn to Marie and Rai as they entered the room   and started asking several students their opinions about the sudden winds and the storm. Eventually they came to the table where Zwick was, sitting with Kent and Whitney. Rai did not talk to Whitney although she was chatting to both Zwick and Kent, and they did not interview her which surprised Zwick. But as the purpose was to collect views for the paper, Whitney did not mind because she had no problems with Rai. However she could not understand why she behaved the way she did.

Finally the lectures were over but Zwick had not yet appeared on campus. Although Rai and Marie tried to look for him they did not find him.

The next day immediately after lunch, Zwick escorted Whitney to the cemetery where her mother was buried. As they made their way to the grave clutching large colorful bouquets, Whitney told Zwick about her mother's early life and the good times they had had before the accident.

On arriving they started cleaning the grave and then placed their flowers on it. Then they moved toward the bench under a shady tree across the cemetery.

"By the way Zwick, who is your date at the campus? You're neither here nor there with me, but seem very close to Marie these days. I know it may seem quite funny my asking you this, but …"

This was an extremely difficult question for Zwick to answer at that moment for he was in reality Whitney's secret admirer.

In the moment of silence that followed while Whitney stood waiting for the answer, Zwick felt his face redden. This question actually put him in a dilemma. Although he was physically strong and mentally agile he was at a loss for words for a moment or two. Then he blurted out….

"I really don't know just now, but I am trying not to worry too much about it. I hope you don't believe any of those baseless rumors," Zwick said as he continued staring at her

Whitney looked abashed on hearing Zwick ' answer. Then, to cover her embarrassment, she immediately suggested they leave as it was getting late.

CHAPTER FIVE

On Marie's birthday a few days later, she had invited most her friends to a party at their hostel. Zwick and Whitney were going to the party together and decided to visit a gift shop nearby to buy their gifts. Zwick bought a teddy bear and Whitney bought a very nice white dress as gifts to surprise Marie on her 20th birthday.

Despite Zwick going to the party with Whitney, he had started regretting the answer he gave her when she asked him whether he had any girlfriend. Being her secret admirer, he felt incapable of expressing his true feelings to Whitney, especially since they had been friends for quite a long time.

When they reached the party, they were received warmly. Zwick was pleasantly surprised to find his other fellows students, including Kent, at the party. Later he realized that Karl was not there. Then, as they were sharing the cake, Marie, whose voice had already become hoarse because of too much cheering, called upon Kent to open the dance officially.

As Kent moved toward the dance floor he called upon Whitney to join him. Whitney accepted willingly enough, happy to dance with Kent because they were friends and she knew him as they were in the same study group. But while they danced, Zwick glared at them in a baleful way. He started sulking to show his disapproval and displeasure at the fact that Whitney was dancing with Kent.

But, as the music played on, Kent felt a little aroused by the pressure of his body against that of Whitney's. When Zwick noticed this he was upset and decided to leave the party by himself.

When the dance had ended, Whitney went looking for Zwick since they had been seated together before the dance but could find him nowhere. Later, Marie came and informed her about his departure as they were dancing. This upset Whitney and she wondered how Zwick could leave without informing her, so she decided to leave herself.

On the way home she tried to call Zwicks' phone but could not get through to him. It wasn't until the next morning when they meet at the campus that they had a chance to speak.

Actually Zwick was trying to avoid her by keeping himself busier than ever. Although Whitney could only guess why Zwick angry with her she also decided to ignore him. This went on for a couple of days and the two friends did not talk to each other.

Zwick had to meet his study group members in the lecture room one day, but immediately after they had finished with the discussions, Matt came and they remained together in the hall until after Rai and Marie had gone.

"Do you know what? And you've got to believe this man, because it's worse than awful," Matt said in a low voice.

"What is it all about?" Zwick asked anxiously.

"I think Kent and Whitney are very serious about each other. They're much closer than they were on Marie's birthday." Matt said.

"And how do you know all that?" Zwick asked him.

"Last night we were in Hard Rock Pub, and I was shocked to

See Whitney and Kent also in the club. They were openly kissing and hugging each other and this went on until they left," Matt continued.

At first Zwick was stunned as he listened in disbelief. The fact was that he was intoxicated by Whitney's beauty and this was driving him crazy. And although his jealousy was now driving them apart he did not want to discuss this with anyone else.

Once in awhile, Whitney did try to meet Zwick after realizing that he also had feelings for her so that they could talk it over.

But things just didn't seem to work out.

One night she came to a new realization. She was on her bed as she groaned, "It's really inevitable for now.I love Kent."

Later the next morning Karl came to the campus, but this time he was quieter than usual. Passing through the compound, he saw some photographs on the notice board and decided to have a look at them. As he moved closer to the board, however, he realized they were the pictures that had been taken at Marie's birthday party when Kent was dancing with Whitney. Obviously he felt displeased as he glanced at the photos,

"This might be serious," Karl muttered under his breath.

He winced at the thought that these shots would have been seen by several students after they were stuck on the notice board.

Later, as soon as the lectures were over, Zwick moved on but was suddenly joined by a fuming Matt.

"We've got to be careful with Kent," Matt said as he walked alongside Zwick.

"Why do you say that?" Zwick asked.

"Whitney told me that you were dating Marie but its Kent who misled her with that piece of information". Matt said

"What?" Zwick asked in shock.

"Well, she said you have strong links with Marie and you deceived her when she asked you about which girl you were dating. So she thinks whatever you said on that day was a lie," Matt said trying to convince Zwick who seemed to think it was a joke.

Zwick was puzzled about these rumors, but although they were not friends and Zwick knew he shouldn't expect too much from Kent, he was upset at

Whitney calling him a liar when it was Kent who was spreading a lot of rumors pretending to be in the know about his relationship with Marie. Despite the fact that Zwick did not really have a relationship with Marie in the first place, what upset him was that Whitney believed his lies. He wondered if this would mark the end of their friendship. He knew that Kent would gloat over him now that he was dating Whitney. What upset him even further was that he would find it difficult to talk to Whitney which would please Kent no end. He hoped, though, that he would still be able to talk to her about their studies and that he could continue helping her academically. And, as it must, time went on. Zwick tried to start a new life with his study group members and with Matt to whom he was growing closer and whom he now felt was a friend.

It was extremely humiliating for Zwick to be forced to watch Kent and Whitney having fun together at the campus, but it was something he couldn't avoid so he tried to take it in his stride. Some times Zwick would feel as if he was only three inches tall because Kent who was once his friend had behaved in this abominable way to separate him from Whitney.

After winning her heart, Kent joined Whitney in signing up for the miming competitions that were to be held at the club. Several other students, including Marie and Rai, entered the competition, too. Unfortunately Zwick missed the mimes as he had started living a lonely life and he really did not wish to see Whitney and Kent together.

Late on the night of the competition Marie and Rai departed from the club. They had eagerly anticipated that Zwick would join them but were disappointed.

Although Kent had misled Whitney with false information about Zwick he did not blame her completely for believing him. In fact, he felt he was partly to blame for not being open with her in the first place when he had the chance to do so.

The next day at university Karl had missed the first lecture but no sooner did he see Whitney as he stood beside his car, than he called out to her. As she approached, Karl made plans with her for them to meet the following day at Eastside Hotel at exactly 6:00pm. Whitney agreed, rather uncertainly though, as she didn't think she was ready to meet him in a public place as yet.

On the appointed day she decided to go before the agreed time since she and Kent were to meet up a little later and she did not want to miss that. Looking around, she saw only a few other people at their tables and could not see Karl anywhere near the hotel.

As she was looking around, a waitress came and led her to an empty table at the side. Whitney kept her eyes focused straight ahead. She then noticed Karl hurrying along because he was late. As they started talking, Whitney requested him to get to the main point as to why he had asked her to meet him there.

"I know this will sound crazy to you, but I have booked two flight tickets for a holiday hoping you will be interested in the offer, and I thought you deserve it," Karl said, not very sure of the outcome but none the less politely.

"Well good luck to you and it's quite interesting, but no, thanks. I will not take up the offer because and I have too many commitments with my dad. But you can still try with someone else since it's not too late for you," she said as she rejected Karl's holiday offer.

Karl was disappointed with her answer as he thought no one could resist such an offer but Whitney had done so. In the moment of awkward silence that followed Whitney's reply he began thinking of what he could do next. Whitney decided to leave but wished him an enjoyable holiday.

"Okay, now I have proved she is in love with him," Karl thought to himself as he remained seated alone at the table after Whitney's departure.

But on leaving the motel Whitney went directly home as her father had gone abroad for a business trip and she had chores to do.

That night Zwick was watching television at home when Matt came visiting with DVD of the miming competition at the club that Zwick had missed. Although he did not expect Matt at that time, Zwick believed he would be interested in the DVD as he hadn't attended the function. Luckily enough Matt had recorded the whole event and they settled down to watch it. Almost immediately Zwick realized that the cameras had focused mainly on Whitney and Kent. This depressed Zwick a great deal because he really adored Whitney even though he always felt too embarrassed and reluctant to let her know.

"You have to try to feel as if nothing ever happened. I know how it hurts if someone you think of is going out with another guy, but you never had any luck with her," Matt said trying to give Zwick a shoulder to lean on.

Karl, in the meantime was deeply frustrated over Whitney's rejection of his offer. He woke up late that morning and began to prepare his breakfast as he was feeling quite hungry. In fact, Karl had started noticing some physical changes in his life ever since he had lost the bangle although he never revealed that secret to any of his friends including the lawyer he always regarded as a relative.

But as he was sitting down that morning, he began day dreaming about how, were he to marry Whitney, she would one day have his son who would inherit his kingdom. He was lost in a world of 'what ifs?' until the alarm of the microwave that he was using to warm breakfast brought him back to the present and to reality.

CHAPTER SIX

Zwick in the meantime had become quite irregular at university. He dreaded facing all his friends who knew of his infatuation with Whitney and who might laugh at him behind his back because they were no longer a couple. Mr. Taji had just returned from a business trip and was planning to introduce Whitney to the Taji Corporation as his daughter who had grown up and was ready to join the company. He had planned that Whitney would take up a top managerial position in the firm on completing her studies. He was certain that she would be an asset to the firm and would bring a lot to it. He knew that only positive things could happen to the firm with Whitney in it.

Karl made a trip to the campus to meet the entertainment official as he wanted more details about the party planned for the end of the semester as he would be away for two weeks and didn't want to miss anything when he returned. While there, as he was moving through the campus, he noticed Whitney and Kent sitting beneath a palm tree. Most of the couple's friends were not in favor of their relationship as they knew it came out of a misunderstanding with Zwick. In fact they had all been witness to a fight between Kent and Zwicks a few days earlier and most of them felt sorry for Zwick. As Karl hung around on some pretext or another he noticed the two love birds leave the campus together.

"What happens if we get engaged immediately after graduation?" Kent asked Whitney as they were moving on.

Despite the fact that they had deep feelings for each other, this question seemed a little difficult for Whitney to answer at that moment. She tried to evade the reply saying that her father always liked her friends,

"I hope my dad will feel happy when he finds out about us because then will be the right time for this sort of stuff," Whitney replied in a few words.

Even though their relationship had started with a lie and with Whitney's indecision, she now believed that God had really had meant them to love each other. Kent had proved to be trust worthy although many of his friends didn't think so, and he had become unpopular with those who sided with Zwick.

As they were exiting through the first gate Whitney and Kent saw Rai and Marie approach the notice board to put up a notice with all the details of the party at the end of the semester.

Whitney and Kent went back to see what they had put on the board. Scanning the board they noticed the names of the drama club members who had been selected to present a comedy. Zwick was also on the list although he was unaware of that since he had not been attending university those last few days.

Whitney later suggested that she go to Zwicks' place to inform him of the program. But this did not please Kent as, feeling a twinge of guilt about all that he had said about Zwick, he was not ready to face him again so soon. Later, though, he did agree to Whitney's suggestion, and they decided to go together to Zwick's place so that they could inform him of the program.

Whitney at times used to wonder about Zwick. She felt guilty about what she had done as Zwick had been a very good friend, one who had been there when she had lost her mother and had made every effort to see that she returned to her normal self after her loss. He had never left her alone in that period and he had always attended his lectures regularly because of her. Whenever she remembered those times she felt a twinge of sympathy for

Zwick although did realize that now she really loved Kent.

Now on this particular evening, Zwick was cleaning up the house since his uncle was expected to return from his holiday very soon. As he was cleaning the wardrobe he noticed a briefcase with a digital lock. He realized he had never ever seen his uncle opening it. Curiosity got the better of him so he carefully set it down on the table and opened it. His eyes widened in surprise as he saw the case was full of guns and boxes of bullets. He had not associated his uncle with these sorts of arms although he knew that Mr. Dean was a Second World War veteran.

He picked up a gun and, seeing that it was dusty blew on it. But as he started doing so, he heard someone knocking on the door. He set the gun down on the table and headed to the door to see who was knocking.

He was quite surprised to see Kent and Whitney. He had almost forgotten about them, not having seen them for quite some time. Seeing them again suddenly brought back a rush of memories, some of them not very pleasant. But, being polite, he invited them in and asked them to make themselves at home. Ever the perfect host, he offered them two glasses of wine as they seated themselves on the sofa.

Then he resumed his cleaning while the gun rested on the table. But his visitors were pretty uncomfortable after they noticed the gun and the bullets on the table. Was Zwick planning to use them, they wondered, and where? In fact Kent was on edge all the time and so he requested Whitney to get to the point so that they could leave as early as possible. If truth be told, he worried a little that Zwick may shoot him in an act of vengeance.

And perhaps this could have been a possibility. Zwick still held a grudge against Kent as he believed he had stolen Whitney from him, and was thinking of just such a possibility at that moment.

Then, when he felt he could no longer control himself he suggested they leave so that he could resume his cleaning.

When they were sure he was gone, Zwick settled

down to some shooting practice with blanks in the back yard.

Much later that night, Whitney was at the dining table with her father,

"Dad, do you know what?" she asked solemnly.

"No," Mr. Taji said kindly.

"I have a very nice friend and he wants to visit you," she summoned enough courage to say, trying to sound as nonchalant as she possibly could.

"A campus mate, huh?" Mr. Taji asked while nodding thoughtfully.

"Yes, Dad and we're finishing the same year, although he is doing a business course," Whitney said.

"Well, daughter, he's welcome to visit any day he wishes to," Mr. Taji replied calmly.

Whitney now knew that now it was up to her to organize her boy friend's visit home. On leaving the dining room she phoned Kent to inform him that she had finished convincing her father.

It was at about this time that Zwick received a telegram from his uncle, Mr. Dean, who was still on holiday in Paris. "How are you doing, son? I know you're great but I just want to let you know I will be returning in a week's time," his uncle said in the telegram.

However, Zwick didn't really feel that great. Neither did he feel like going to the campus that day and decided to stay at home. He sent a reply to his uncle telling him that every thing, including his studies, was fine. In reality, though, Zwick was now spending more time at home watching movies. And in between them he spent time looking at pictures of Whitney and mourning over them and what could have been. He began realizing how much he had suffered since Whitney and he had parted ways.

Then came the day when Kent made up his mind to go to Whitney's' home to meet Mr. Taji. All through the long afternoon Whitney moved about anxiously, waiting for Kent to arrive.

When he did finally arrive, Whitney felt relieved for she had half feared he would let her down and would not visit.

He had been there before, once earlier when Mr. Taji had been away, and so things looked fairly familiar the second time round. Whitney welcomed him happily and led him into the sitting room where Mr. Taji was sitting at his computer.

CHAPTER SEVEN

"Hello! I have an assignment for you." Matt gazed at the email from a well to do merchant offering him a deal. "I'll pay you $60,000 in cash if you're ready to do my job."

Although Matt had been secretly working as an assassin for some time now, he had never considered himself to be so expensive and had never been offered that much money as payment before. "I know there are quite a few who are good at this kind of job but I require an extra smart one this time. So if you're interested, contact me at your earliest. This is the picture of the person in question," the mail went on.

At first, Matt had not noticed that the picture sent to him was of Kent, his schoolmate. He began to wonder if some one was trying to trick him by offering him such a large amount of money. What worried him even more was how they had learned he was an assassin. He wondered how the writer had learned of him and how he could contact him. He did not really like assignments from people he did not know and would not be at peace until he knew the answers to his questions.

On taking a second look at the picture and realizing it was indeed Kent he was quite taken aback. He had been asked to finish the job at the party at the end of the semester.

As he studied the check for $60,000 he mulled over it even more. At this time, his main interest was not to get on with the killing but to find out who had sent him that money.

His first thoughts went to Zwick, which under the

circumstances, was quite understandable. But he knew Zwick would not be able to raise that amount whatever it took.

"Oh my God, I can't believe this! What the hell did Kent do that this guy wants him dead?" Matt asked himself.

"I will seek confirmation that you will do the job within 24 hours," were the last few words in the message.

Interrupted by a sudden movement, he turned his head to see Marie entering. She sat on the sofa beside Matt's computer,

"Oh, I'm... How are you? How is Rai?" Matt stuttered trying to close down the page which on which he was communicating with his anonymous client and opening other pages.

"May I have a look at that?" Marie requested.

She insisted but without touching the cursor. At first Matt was afraid thinking that Marie had already seen what was on the page he had just closed.

Matt had managed to keep the secret of him being an assassin for hire to himself for several years. But now he knew that if Marie had seen the page, his secret would be discovered. Luckily enough, though, Marie was more interested in opening up some other pages which she studied closely.

"Have you seen these scholarships before?" she asked Matt excitedly.

"Yes, but I have already been selected. Besides, the last date for any applications has expired and they aren't taking any more. Tough luck," Matt replied.

Marie felt happy about these scholarships because she saw that they were being offered by some of the best known universities in the world.

Seeing that Marie was more concerned with other things rather than with what he had been looking at, Matt breathed a sigh of relief. Up to now he had never been threatened by the chance of someone discovering his secret. However close one was to him he had not revealed the fact of his being a gun- for- hire to anyone.

Back again at the computer he glanced at Marie and saw her engrossed in a magazine. He turned the monitor so that Marie could not see it from where she was sitting. Claiming that that he was busy, Matt turned back to his client's page to finish the deal. He was surprised to see that the mystery man had tried to contact him on Yahoo Messenger.

Acknowledging him, Matt queried of his anonymous new client, "When do you really need that job done?"

"The best option would be on the day of the campus party," replied the client.

"You will have to pay me more than what you have offered so far, though, because this is high profile and is going to be quite tricky," Matt replied. "Or else I suggest you try someone else."

"Well I will think about it," said the anonymous client and ended the conversation.

A short time later, Matt escorted Marie back to her hostel. Then he hurried home to check his e-mails.

He was pleased to read the client's cryptic message: "Fine. I have the money. Make it happen."

Matt looked around him. $60,000 was really some big cash and there were plenty of things he could do with that kind of money.

But, for some reason he couldn't put a finger on, he was apprehensive about the job. He thought about how the police would track him, and put a ransom on his head and finally trace him.

This kept him preoccupied for quite some time and for the first time in a long, long while he was in two minds about whether he should take up the job or not. He also worried about the fact that he knew the intended victim but had no idea who the client was.

A week passed by during which time Matt heard the rumor that Kent had visited Mr. Taji and had informed him that he intended to marry Whitney after their graduation. This set Matt to wondering whether Mr. Taji was his client, and the last email sort of confirmed it.

"Yeah' I think it's him," he muttered to himself, "but why does he want him dead?"

He groaned thoughtfully. Matt had actually faced Mr. Taji just once in his life. It was when they had gone to visit Ms Darien when she was sick before her death.

Eventually Matt was convinced that Mr. Taji was the client. It had to be. The coincidences were too compelling. He felt a little better about things now that he knew who he was dealing with. He now knew that he was dealing with the richest man in Green Oasis, he was sure he would be paid, and he knew who he could turn to in case things went wrong.

"I will meet you and after that I think you will be able to do the job in the specified time." It was an email from Mr. Taji. As Matt stared at the email, he thought of living a very luxurious life with Marie and the money he would receive for killing Kent.

Matt always liked to surprise Marie, and this time he imagined how he was going to buy her a brand new car so that she could drive herself to the campus in it like Whitney did.

Looking at the clock Matt saw that it was 2a.m. in the morning and he was still dreaming about how he would spend all that money as he lay down on his bed. While thinking of the consequences of his sudden wealth he also worried about Zwick asking him where he had got the money from.

Marie would want to know, too. Marie's family wasn't well off and she had spent most of her childhood and adolescence in a convent under the care of the sisters there. It was while still thinking of the difficult life he himself had gone through that Matt decided to go ahead, carry out the assignment and kill his classmate. Now that he knew what he was going to do, he finally fell into a somewhat restless sleep.

As the sun rose the next morning, Matt jumped out of his bed although he still felt sleepy and unrested. He immediately thought of the appointment he had made with Mr. Taji the previous night and readied himself to meet him at the Oasis Theatre so that they could finalize the deal and he could pick up the first installment from Whitney's father.

Matt thought about how his wealth would command respect at the university in the same way that the wealthy Kent's did. Being a working person, although a student at Green Oasis University, Kent always had money with him and made sure those around him knew he did.

Karl, too, had his followers. Most of the students feared him because of his family background and its evil reputation. Matt wondered if, one day, he would have his gang of fans, too.

He took his time walking towards the building where Mr. Taji would be waiting. Trying to appear nonchalant he moved on, determined not to let Mr. Taji see that he was somewhat afraid and concerned.

A group of actors were rehearsing in one corner of the theater but there was no sign of Mr. Taji. This surprised him because he had expected to find him already there. He did, however, notice a man somewhat similar to Mr. Taji lurking in the shadows but he could not be too sure because it had been a long time since he had met him at his home.

As the minutes passed and there were no developments he decided to enter the hall and look around once more. It was then that he looked at his watch and realized that he was early for the appointment.

"Matt?" he suddenly heard what sounded like Mr. Taji calling in his distinguished voice.

The voice continued calling out to Matt but as he could see no one, peer as he might into the darkness, he grew a little wary. He turned toward where the voice could have come from and, not really being able to see anything, started toward the reception counter in front of him.

He was disappointed to see that Mr. Taji was nowhere near the counter. He craned his neck and peered into the recesses behind the counter but saw nobody. He did, however, become aware of a black briefcase.

Examining it he found it to be locked. He looked all around to see if there was anyone to whom the suitcase could belong when suddenly he was startled by the ringing of his cell phone. Carefully looking around and reaching the spot where the brief case was   he pulled out the phone from his pocket and held it to his ear.

"Hello, hello?" Matt started calling repeatedly for some time, but no one answered him.

Then he heard it. A low, rasping voice which was obviously being disguised, almost whispered, "Have you discovered the brief case yet?"

"Where are you?" Matt asked, replying with a question which he knew instinctively would not be answered.

The mystery speaker instructed Matt to pick up the brief case, which he did. The voice on the other end then told him he was being paid the full amount to encourage him to accomplish the task successfully. Anxiously, Matt looked all around to see whether there was anyone else in the place and when he has finally made sure that he was alone in the place, tried opening the briefcase. With his heart thudding in his ears, he opened it with the code he was then given. Barely able to breathe he looked at the money and shuffled through it confirming it was $80,000, the final decided amount. Then he noticed it- a photograph, face down. Turning it over, Matt saw the familiar face of Kent grinning up at him. The sight of Kent almost made him gag.

His next worry was how he was going to get out of the building, unnoticed. What if someone in authority confronted him and found him with so much money? How could he explain it? Carefully, he tried to cover the case with a newspaper from the counter. Then he started moving towards the exit door with his precious parcel.

CHAPTER EIGHT

Whitney was woken by the hot rays of the afternoon sun shining through the windows. Tossing about on her bed, she made a mental note to draw the shades in future. Looking at her watch she saw it was 4 o'clock, late enough for her to have to get up, but early enough for her to linger in bed a little longer. After lingering some more, she checked her voice mail and then got of bed. She reminded herself that she would have to prepare supper for her father before she left for the party on the campus, and she set about it almost immediately.

After washing up she went to her father's room to say her goodbyes and found him almost dressed to go out himself, fitting a shoe on his left foot.

"So, will all your friends be attending the party tonight?" he asked Whitney.

"Yes dad," she replied with a tinge of excitement in her voice.

"You take care of your self daughter," Mr. Taji said as he exited through the main door.

Almost immediately Whitney set about readying herself for the party. As she put on her white party dress her mind went back to Kent and their relationship. Did she really love him, she wondered. She knew she trusted him. He had proved himself faithful despite the false information about him spread by Zwick and Matt. But perhaps this was his way of proving his love for her and of keeping Zwick out of the picture and at a distance from her. Her thoughts went to how he had visited her father, a sign that he was serious about her. Did she visualize a future with Kent, she asked herself. Perhaps she did, was the reply she received.

It was while she was cross examining herself that Kent arrived to pick her up.

They drove out to the campus and headed for the hall where the party was to be held. The place was crowded with students who would be graduating as well as their guests. The campus looked like a fairyland all lit up with beautiful lights and with buntings and balloons everywhere, proclaiming the festive spirit of the evening. Music pulsated through the windows and out the doors onto the sultry summer air, punctuated by loud and raucous laughter.

Kent entered the hall with Whitney on his arm only to find the celebrations had already begun. They made such a pretty picture that all the students turned to stare at them. As they looked around for their seats Whitney noticed many of the students admiring the gorgeous necklace she wore around her neck which made her quite uncomfortable. In her hand Whitney held the blood red rose Lisa had handed her a little earlier. It had accompanied a note from Karl wishing them luck for the future. Whitney accepted it as a sign that Karl had finally acknowledged her relationship with Kent and was relieved.

Luckily Whitney and Kent did find a couple of seats and Whitney was glad for the opportunity to move away from the spotlight.

Looking around her, Whitney spotted many of her fellow classmates, Rai, Lisa, Marie and a host of others. Whitney wondered about Zwick and whether he would be there that evening. Somehow, she was sure he would. After everything had quietened down and the opening prayers led by Marie were said, the master of ceremonies welcomed them. Whitney noticed Karl entering the hall which surprised her because she thought he was still away on holiday.

The master of ceremonies then called Karl to the dais to deliver the end of semester holiday massage.

Karl's speech done, the master of ceremonies called upon the drama group, which was supposed to be led by Zwick, to do their thing. Unfortunately Zwick had not bothered to attend the rehearsals at the campus but the administration didn't know about it. As every one looked at the stage expectantly, it gradually sank in that Zwick was not at the function at that moment. And in the uncomfortable silence that prevailed Kent and Whitney also noticed that Zwick was not at the function, which surprised them because he had taken it upon himself to inform them about the function. Some of the audience hoped it was only a matter of being held up somewhere and that he would turn up any moment. But he didn't and eventually the troupe began their act without him.

Increasingly frustrated with the situation, Rai moved out of the hall with her video camera without filming anything although she had been anxious to cover the party while Marie was at the refreshment table. She was already bored with the function although it had just started, and she moved on.

Now that the formalities were over the fun part began. Music throbbed, most couples danced while some made a beeline to the refreshments and some went outside for a breath of fresh air and to be by themselves.

It was at about this time that Zwick was at home seemingly preparing him self for a journey and not for the party at the campus,

Back at the campus Rai was also seen sitting alone at the end of the building opposite to the entertainment hall, looking extremely unhappy.

As the party progressed Kent and Whitney were voted the best couple of the day which surprised many at the campus who had not known of their relationship. They joined the other couples on the dance floor.

"Indeed, this is the happiest day in my life and this is truly a great party," said Whitney to Kent as they started dancing. On the floor they met many of their friends, all of whom appeared very happy for the two of them.

In the meantime Marie moved out to look for Rai but as she was looking around the compound she noticed Karl and Lisa walking across the parking lot.

"Hey, have you seen Rai around?" Marie asked them.

"Sorry, no. We've just come out of the hall, too," Lisa said as they moved away.

Marie continued scouring the grounds for Rai as she moved towards the main campus entrance. As she neared the gate, she noticed a car parked nearby. It appeared to be similar to Zwicks' but Marie did not bother to check who was inside due to the fact that she had not seen Zwick right from the beginning of the party. Moreover, and really surprisingly, although this car was similar to Zwicks', this one had no registration number and all the window glasses were tinted black making it difficult for any one to see who the driver was.

As Marie continued her search for Rai she realized that her phone was off so she switched it on again and tried Rai's number several times, unsuccessfully. It was now 6.00pm, the party was at its peak and Marie had not yet been able to contact Rai.

Suddenly there was a power breakage. Since it had been unexpected, no one had thought of candles or lamps, and everything was plunged in total darkness. There was silence in the hall as the sound systems were quietened too. Nobody could tell why the power had gone off as this had never happened before in the history of Green Oasis University. The students looked at each other, sheepish and disappointed.

Suddenly there was the sharp rat-a-tat of a machine gun being fired directly into the dance hall. For a moment there was a stunned silence and then the air was rent with frightened screams. One could hear the voices of different people crying for help from all the corners of Green Oasis University. Chaos and confusion reigned.

Almost as suddenly, a few minutes later, though it did seem like hours to the frightened students, there was the even louder sound of scores of police alarms, sirens and emergency ambulances and a flash of light from a helicopter hovering overhead.

The police tried to cordon off the whole area, in the hope of preventing the shooter from escaping and the medical team rushed directly to the dance hall. But they were too late. The entire floor had already turned red with the blood bath. In their search for survivors in the hall, it was only Kent who was found still breathing. He was rendered immediate help and put on a respirator but the doctors felt his chances of survival were very slim considering the number of times he had been shot and the amount of blood he had lost.

Kent was rushed directly to hospital for an emergency operation while other medical workers remained behind collecting the bodies of the other students and their identity cards. All the students in the hall were declared dead and Whitney, the only daughter to Mr. Taji, was among the rest who had not survived the frenzied shootings.

This situation at Green Oasis became unbearable as many who were outside the hall continued to mourn around the campus. This was the most terrible thing that had ever happened in Green Oasis. Those who had survived were absolutely inconsolable and moved around the campus dazedly.

The police were still searching for the gunman but neither he nor any weapon had been discovered as yet. The police chief and his posse started approaching different students in the compound wanting to find out how they had organized their party right from the beginning. They failed to elicit anything really worth while. Most of the students were too afraid and too shocked to really be of much help.

Then one of them approached Marie who was shivering and moaning on a bench under the umbrella tree. She looked totally spaced out and unaware of what was happening around her. But for the fact that Marie had moved out of the hall to look for Rai she would have been among the victims of the frenzy shooting was not lost on her. In fact it made her cry all the more because she had survived by a hair's breath. She had not been able to believe her eyes when she saw Whitney's body lying in a pool of blood that had turned her white dress red. Marie was so stunned that for a moment she wondered whether it had all been an act and her friends had been shooting a movie scene. But that would not have called for as many medical staff as she had seen on the campus.

"Hello, young girl, I feel sorry about this and I know it is really heart breaking but I wanted to ask you a few questions regarding what went on here tonight," said the sheriff, breaking Marie's concentration.

At first Marie did not seem to hear the sheriff and she felt as though someone was talking to her from very far away. Then, slowly, she looked up and noticed the sheriff standing in front of her less than a meter away. But she remained silent, unable to answer him.

"Come on, young lady," the sheriff urged while chewing the end of his pencil, pad in hand.

Again Marie did not say anything at all because so she was so terrified about what had happened on the campus.

It was at about the same time that Zwick had gone to collect his uncle, Mr. Dean, home from the airport back from his holiday in Paris and was driving him home. Both of them seemed to be unaware of what was happening at the campus.

Meanwhile, back at the campus the sheriff was continuing his interrogation of Marie. "Do you know some of other students who didn't attend the party?" he asked.

After a few seconds Marie nodded her head in response to what the sheriff had asked her.

"Can I get their names?" the sheriff inquired of her.

Marie wasn't able to hold her tears back as she mentioned Zwick.

"What were the relationships among the various students like?" the sheriff continued his probe.

"Well, Whitney, one of those victims shot in the hall, actually had a few misunderstandings with Zwick, but before that they were good friends. They split up after one of their group mates fell in love with her. It was then that Zwick stopped talking to Whitney and her fiancé Kent, the young man who survived the shooting in the hall," Marie explained painfully through her copious tears.

By this time many relatives of the students were at the campus, among them Mr. Taji who secretly believed that the killer he had hired had missed his target killing his own daughter while Kent, whom he wanted dead had survived and was now in hospital.

"This damn well messed up the whole deal, and now my daughter is dead," Mr. Taji muttered to himself as he sat in his car.

Later the chancellor announced the closure of the university until further notice. He tried to address the hostile and angry relatives of students as well as he could but they were in no mood to be comforted.

It was a short time later that the police discovered Karl in a car in the parking lot. He was bleeding as he had been shot in the arm but was still alive. Lisa, however, had not been so lucky. She was seated in the front seat of Karl's car, shot in the forehead and already dead. Karl was rushed to the hospital. He was the second of the only two survivors found.

Defeated, Mr. Taji drove home with a heavy heart several hours later.

As he opened the front door he was surprised to see the briefcase which he had given to Matt near it. He approached the briefcase warily suspecting it may be booby trapped. Then, he reached down to examine it more closely and noticed a hand written note beside it. This surprised him greatly and curiosity got the better of him as he picked up the note and proceeded to read what Matt had written.

"I'm sorry Mr. Taji. I was too late to do the job. I found it already done by someone else when I arrived there. I am so sorry to hear about your daughter's death. I am returning your money and I wish you the best."

Mr. Taji then opened the briefcase and examined its contents closely. He counted the money and noticed that it was intact. He now thought that Matt had decided to play games with his daughter's life.

"If he didn't, then who did this to my daughter?" he asked himself aloud.

Then he decided to get in touch with the police and assist them in whatever way he could to identify the person who had killed his daughter. He found it ironical that he had hired an assassin to kill Kent who was dating his daughter, but surprisingly it was only Kent who survived the shooting although he was still in a coma, and his beloved daughter was dead.

Zwick was chatting with his uncle over breakfast the next morning when the doorbell rang. On opening the door Mr. Dean saw two men smartly dressed up black suits, introducing themselves as CID agents. Despite the fact that Zwick was at the airport at the time when the party was underway at the campus, the visitors revealed that they considered him a suspect for the frenzied shooting based on the fact that his car was seen at the main entrance. Besides, according to several students Zwick had had misunderstandings with Whitney who had died on the spot in the hall. Mr. Dean was at a loss as to how Zwicks' car could have been seen parked outside the campus when he had driven him home in it at the same time things were happening at the university, and as the offices took Zwick away he immediately telephoned his lawyer.

As far as he could recall, Zwick had been with him from the time he had met him at the airport. In fact he had been waiting for him at the airport even before that which is why he had missed the party altogether, They had both had been unaware about the shooting that had occurred at the campus, even when the campus was closed down after the event.

The news channels were camped outside the university, busy reporting every little piece of information they could garner. Now they were airing the news that the police had one suspect who they believed could be responsible for murdering his fellow students at Green Oasis University in custody. They were not too sure and it hadn't been confirmed as yet, but the rumor was that he was named Zwick. Detained by the police, Zwick, in the meantime, claimed that he was innocent about what he was being accused of.

At the hospital, Kent was still in a coma and Karl was showing signs of regaining conscious. There was always an officer by his bedside waiting for the opportunity to interrogate him at the earliest. When he opened his eyes for the first time since the incident they were waiting there and did not let the chance to question him pass by.

Unfortunately Karl worsened things for Zwick, as he identified Zwick as the killer responsible for murdering the students at Green Oasis University. He also claimed that Zwick had shot him and Lisa even before going to the hall. Lisa had died on the spot, but he had been in too much of a hurry to get to the hall to notice that Karl had only been shot in the arm and chest and had not died. This statement made Karl the official eye witness to the shooting and he declared he was prepared to bear witness in front of a jury in court.

As a result of Karl's statement Zwick, although innocent, was taken into custody, and charged with committing the massacre.

In jail, Zwick believed it was the end for him because his uncle would not be able to get him released so easily. Zwicks' family was very poor and did not have the resources to hire a top lawyer or to pay his bail. It was because of their poverty that he had grown up living with his uncle. He thought of Madam Tabitha who had told him that he would be lucky all his life but even though he had supernatural powers he found they could not help him this time.

Zwick grew increasingly frustrated in prison as the days passed. Mr. Dean tried to convince the media of his nephew's innocence but his efforts didn't seem to have much of an impact. It was unthinkable to him that his nephew could be found guilty of multiple murders and face the death penalty, more so because he knew he was innocent.

CHAPTER NINE

After a month in jail, Zwick was set to appear in the court of Green Oasis. It was to be his first hearing and by this time even Mr. Taji was convinced that Zwick, the killer he had hired, had not done the job even though Karl said that he had seen Zwick committing the crime. In the face of all the allegations against him, Zwick wondered why Karl tried to accuse him of murder when he was not even at the party.

On the day of the first hearing the court was packed with friends and relatives of the murdered students. As the hearing was about to start the court clerk briefed the audience about the case details and the behavior expected of them and then the proceedings began. Lawyers for both sides, the plaintiffs and the defendant, were present. Everyone was interested in Karl seated in the first row behind the prosecutor and waited anxiously to hear his testimony. But Mr. Dean and his attorney believed they had collected enough evidence to satisfy the jury about Zwicks' innocence in the crime. There was a hushed silence and everyone listened with bated breath as witness after witness was called to the stand to testify.

Although Zwicks' lawyer seemed capable and was well prepared he paled in comparison to the brilliant and theatrical public prosecutor.

Karl, of course, was the center of attention as, in a low but controlled voice, he narrated the events of that fateful day. The only times when his voice quivered and he showed emotion were when he spoke about how Lisa had been shot point blank and when he showed the jury those awful reminders of that fateful day, his scars. He impressed the jury with his calm, collected manner and the onlookers were so affected by what he said that it was only the presence of the officials there that prevented them from lynching Zwick on the spot.

Mr. Taji himself, who really knew it wasn't Zwick who had committed the crimes, and who himself had committed the crime of plotting another's death was so caught up in the heat of the moment that he too began to believe Zwick deserved death for the crimes.

Zwick was taken back to prison by the police after the session. By now he was so concerned about his uncle who seemed to grow more gaunt each time he saw him, that his own concerns and the predicament he was in seemed of secondary importance.

Because he had known Zwick from the time he was a kid and had watched him grow into a fine upstanding man Mr. Dean could not believe anything that was said against Zwick. He felt pretty desperate that the authorities did not believe him when he stated as often as he could that Zwick had been at the airport with him and consequently could not have committed the misdeed. Mr. Dean was now determined more than ever to do whatever would be necessary to prove this.

What really went against Zwick was the fact that several witnesses thought they had seen Zwick in his car parked at the gate, and what made things more suspicious was the fact that the car did not have any registration plates.

This dashed the hopes of Mr. Dean of rescuing Zwick although he knew Zwick had been framed. He knew it would now be extremely difficult to clear his name.

Finally the long awaited day for most of the people in Green Oasis town arrived. It was to be the Day of Judgment. For Zwick, there were too many moments of realization that this would be the day on which he was going to be finally found guilty or innocent. Not surprisingly, due to the long time that he had already spent in jail, he felt all was lost and no matter how much his uncle tried to assure him that the truth would emerge he was resigned to the idea that he would be found guilty.

The courtroom was packed to its full capacity and many disappointed hopefuls were turned away at the door. There was an expectant atmosphere and a busy buzz of people murmuring to each other in the room. Then there was a hush as the judge entered and Zwick was brought in.

Zwick had taken care to dress well and present a positive picture to the judge, the jury and to the public on this fateful day. He stole several glances at the audience which included many students from his university. He recognized Rai in the sea of faces, most of whom were nothing more than part of a blurred picture. She was seated in the front row beside a friend whom Zwick seemed to remember vaguely. She looked at Zwick and then lowered her eyes. If truth be told she felt quite sorry for him and realized at that moment how sure she was that Zwick was innocent. And she was not the only one who felt this way. There were many of those in the crowd who deep down in their hearts believed in Zwicks' innocence, too. Even those who perhaps had a lingering suspicion that perhaps he was guilty felt sorry for him and hoped the sentence would not be too harsh.

Mr. Taji was given a place of importance and he showed no sign of copassion for Zwick as he glared at him from behind his spectacles.

Then the judge called the court to order and thus began the day of reckoning. The lawyers from both teams summed up their cases and after the presentations Zwick weighed what he had heard and tried to predict the verdict.

Later, after both sides had finished their summations, the judge was about to send the jury off to the jury room when he looked up and saw Rai raise her hand to attract his attention. Everyone looked enquiringly at Rai, wondering what this could be about, when the judge called upon her to state her point. Standing up, Rai opened the hand bag she had come with, and slowly took out her video camera. It was the same one she had had at the party.

Holding it aloft, Rai told the court, "Now it's time to face the truth. I've been silent for so long because I was afraid. But I realize now there has to be this moment. I simply cannot let it pass me by."

As she walked towards the judge to hand in the video camera with the recorded evidence about the campus murder Karl requested a short break. However his request was denied by the judge who decided that everyone was supposed to see the last evidence on the camera.

While Karl returned to his seat he looked at Rai with a glum face, his jaws clamped together. Rai ignored him. She was not afraid because she knew the truth. The jury was first given the opportunity to view the evidence and when they had finished viewing it the visitors were shown it, too.

For the first time in the last few days Zwick saw a glimmer of hope and prayed that this new piece of evidence would help the truth be revealed and he would be vindicated.

When it was done the silence in the courtroom was deafening. Then there was pandemonium and it took a whole eleven seconds for the judge and the court officials to bring things under control.

Immediately a warrant was issued for the arrest of Karl, the very same Karl who had figured as the official witness in the case against Zwick; the same Karl who had no compunction about having his friend convicted for something he himself was guilty of.

But everyone present had now seen for themselves how Karl had parked the car and then turned round and cold-bloodedly shot Lisa at point blank range. The camera had followed him as he got out of the car, first hid behind a huge tree in the compound and then gradually made his way to the grounds and from there to the hall. It was as he neared the main entrance to the hall that the lights went out and everything was plunged into complete darkness. The camera was able to catch the faint outline of Karl as he aimed his gun at the crowd and started shooting aimlessly. The camera caught the orange red spark of each bullet as it left the weapon but they came so fast and so furious that they merged into one another and looked more like tongues of burning flame.

Behind the camera that day, Rai had all but lost her nerve. Her instinct was to run but she called upon every ounce of courage in her body and continued filming, unbeknown to Karl, from the shelter of a nearby tree.

It was all she could do from screaming, but her camera had picked up how, after the shooting, Karl had run back to his car and, without even glancing at Lisa, swallowed a pill and then lay back, waiting for unconsciousness to take over.

The police had found him alive but in a coma, and he had been rushed to the hospital which he left the next day after a quick recovery.

This had been a time of great sorrow for the town of Green Oasis; an absolutely heart breaking time as people mourned the loss of their relatives and loved ones, and the jury remembered it vividly.

There was not a dry eye in the jury box as Zwick was now declared free to leave while Karl was arrested and charged with the multiple murders. The death penalty now seemed imminent for him.

Zwick and his uncle hugged each other and laughed and cried with relief and the joy of Zwick being free once more. Then they embraced Rai and thanked her over and over again for delivering Zwick from certain death.

As for Karl, he was all but forgotten in the celebrations and only a handful of people noticed him being led way and entering the police van.

"The son is evil like his parents, and now he will pay for his and their evil ways," called an elderly gentleman after the moving van.

Surprisingly, Karl did not look the least bit

remorseful for his deeds nor the least bit perturbed by the turn of events although he knew that he would, most likely have to face the death punishment. As the van started moving, he waved at Rai through the window and laughed at her discomfort.

Karl was pronounced dead on a Monday, at 5:35pm, twenty minutes after he was executed a week later.

The few people who witnessed his execution did report, though, that he no longer was the arrogant grinning person they had seen at the courthouse. He appeared more subdued as he spoke out for the last time in his life.

"What's happening to me right now is unjust and the system has failed me," he said to those who would listen.

"Your hearts are bad, and your eyes don't see correctly, but we shall meet again," he continued with a tremor in his voice that had not been there as far back as anyone could remember.

This was not the first time that capital punishment was being meted out. In fact it was the fourth in that many number of years and opinions about it varied greatly. The fact that it was Karl who was to be executed made the issue even more debatable. The people of Green Oasis were aware of his family background and the evil that had been perpetuated by it. They remembered their evil powers, how they had affected so many of their lives adversely and how his parents had met with a fiery death as a response to their subjugation of the local people.

The morning following the execution the streets of Green Oasis were flooded with thousands of people with varying emotions.

Few sympathized with Karl. They were but a handful from those who usually rejected capital punishment outright. Most were relieved by the final verdict and believed Karl's death would finally put an end to this family's evil once and for all. It was as if a cloak of fear had fallen off their shoulders and they spoke more freely and openly with no fear of retaliation, about the family's wickedness and how it had affected them to some degree or another.

CHAPTER TEN

Almost a month later, Green Oasis University reopened with a memorial ceremony to those who had fallen on that terrible day. A memorial stone marked with the names of all the students who had been killed was set up and both, parents and students, paid their respects as the chancellor read the names of the dead, in what would become an annual ritual at the university. With heads bowed, fighting back their tears and holding photographs of their beloved dead, relatives listened as the grim roll call was read out.

"We come together as students and families of Green Oasis University to remember the souls of those who can't be replaced and to share the loss that can't be weighed and to feel their pain," the Chancellor said in his speech.

As soon as the commemoration was over, Zwick went directly to meet those of his friends who were still there that day, especially Rai who had saved him from certain death and then he returned to the place he called home and to Mr. Dean.

"You're quite amazing too," Zwick was reading a note he had received that day. Things were looking up for him now and he was beginning to feel better after a long, long time. He smiled to himself as he folded the note and slipped it into a book he was reading.

And he was not he only one smiling over a note that day.

"My, you look happy," Marie remarked when she

found Rai smiling over one that same day. "Who's the secret admirer?"

Startled, Rai turned to seeing Marie, her roommate sitting besides her on the bed. "Oh, it's nothing" she said shyly.

Rai was secretive by nature and usually hid her feelings from her room mate but this time Marie would not give up that easily.

"Come on, let me know," Marie insisted but Rai hesitated for she knew what could happen if she let Marie know.

It was common knowledge that Marie was an incurable gossip and no secret was safe with her.

"What is it?" she persisted.

"I don't know. I just feel happy today," Rai replied.

Meanwhile, Mr. Taji himself was facing his own ghosts. He explained to those who would listen, and there were quite a number of those, including the sheriff, about the night mares he was experiencing in which Karl's entity featured quite prominently.

"I have seen his corpse with my eyes. Believe me, the way his eyes and heart were plucked from his body reminds me of something I saw when his parents still lived here. And then, there is this statement, the one this entity wrote in blood on the wall. They keep appearing in my nightmares," Mr. Taji would relate.

At first the sheriff thought that Mr. Taji was just reliving the past when Karl's family still held sway over Green Oasis town. But when the narratives became more frequent and more persistent he began to wonder whether they were not just nightmares and whether there was more to them.

In fact, he had no immediate way of stopping this before it went out of control, and he had to respect Mr. Taji what with him being one of the wealthiest and most respected men in their town.

"And I might be the next target of this entity according to the message in my nightmares, and remember he killed my daughter so now you must provide me with enough security at home because I'm very fearful," Mr. Taji confessed.

In fact Mr. Taji had aged all too quickly after the death of his daughter Whitney, and had become extremely introverted and preoccupied.

"But don't rely so much on dreams," the sheriff pleaded with Mr. Taji who was seated at his table, growing increasingly worried about the entity and waiting for the sheriff's conclusion to the matter.

"Ok, it will be alright. We'll take care of it," the Sheriff eventually said and Mr. Taji finally drove off.

That evening, Marie returned to the hostel room she shared with Rai a little later than usual.

"I've got to have a shower first," she informed Rai as she headed straight for the shower. But as soon as she started to shower and feel the warm water cascade over her body, it suddenly turned extremely hot and started scalding her body. She started screaming and immediately turned the shower off. Checking the meter in the bathroom, she found it was fixed at the normal temperature. Standing stranded in the bathroom, she was looking around when something crashed through the shower door, shattering the glass. Marie cowered in the corner in fear. Then, when all was still for a moment and the terror seemed to have passed, she slowly and fearfully ventured out of the shower. She was in total panic, though, as she opened her door a sliver and peeped out. The passage was empty but she did notice there was one door open, and light from it streamed brightly into the corridor. Suddenly a huge black shadow swept over the ceiling, and she immediately closed her door.

Suddenly the doorbell buzzed and she was surprised to find Matt standing at the door. Marie had not really been expecting any one.

"Matt were you here before?" she asked him.

"Oh, no, I've just come in," Matt replied.

"Some one has been here," Marie said, really

terrified.

The next morning, Zwick drove directly to his uncle's paddock for his house keeping. Within an hour, Matt phoned him.

"Hello, Matt," he answered.

"I'm so scared; I have just heard some reports in town about the appearance of Karl's entity. It's already killed his lawyer. It's said his heart and both eyes were plucked out, which is why most of the people believe that it's this entity which did this. This morning the police have issued notices that everybody should remain indoors and inform the police if they notice anything unusual," Matt stuttered on the phone.

"This is really impossible. How could it be? Those are damn rumors Matt, because according to what I know, all the evil powers that belonged to that family were destroyed a long time back. And my uncle told me that the elders committee said the bangle which had those powers had been thrown back into the middle of ocean where his family got it from in the first place. So I just can't believe this, but if it's true it will be difficult to annihilate that evil spell in this town," Zwick continued fretfully. "They always eliminated such culprits as they did his parents, but why has the terror reemerged with so much vengeance?"

Matt finally ended the conversation on the telephone with Zwick, but not without Zwick agreeing to meet Matt at the Hard Rock Pub with Rai.

And that is where the three of them net up that night. Marie and Rai started guzzling beers as Matt and Zwick went to play pool at the table.

"The place is so quiet. I need some music," Rai said.

Trying to appear brave but still sounding shaky and insecure, Marie replied, "I know what you're trying to bring up now."

But Rai went on to the juke box where she played a love ballad. Marie had heard rumors that Rai was now dating Zwick. She had seen them kissing passionately after the memorial ceremony so she believed the rumors to be true. In fact, the pair now seemed inseparable on the campus.

She and Rai continued talking, drinking and laughing. Then Rai called on Zwick to join her despite the fact that he was busy playing pool with Matt. Zwick eventually joined Rai and at one point they started gazing at each other romantically in front of Marie although she did not seem to care at all. Then they started walking around as a couple in the pub, but when he looked at the table where he had left Matt, he was not there.

He requested Rai to hold on and rushed outside the pub looking for Matt. Heading straight to the car park he saw Matt in trouble, fighting with a gang of big guys who were obviously bikers.

Immediately Zwick joined in the fray alongside Matt who seemed to be getting the worse of things just then.

Surprised at the turn of events, the bearded bikers paused their attack and gaped at Zwick who had emerged from nowhere and started kicking their asses. Soon the bikers were on their knees, lowering their heads.

Matt laughed and mocked at them. Then he realized that what he had just seen confirmed his suspicions that Zwick really had super natural powers. There was no other explanation for the way he managed to subdue this large gang of sturdy men.

Hardly had the showdown ended when Rai came out looking for Zwick. It was getting late for her and she and Marie had to return to the hostel. Stepping down the stairs, she moved directly to the parking lot, where she met Zwick.

Marie went off with Matt while she got into Zwicks' car.

Shortly after they had left the pub, as they were still on the way to the hostel, it started raining.

"Have a good night," Rai said as she stepped out of

the car.

By the time Zwick had dropped Rai at the gate a storm had developed and she made her way to the hostel door in pouring rain, overwhelmed by the thunder and lightning.

Marie had already arrived and they soon settled down for the night.

But during the wee hours Rai was suddenly and inexplicably awoken by something dreadful.

She started screaming frantically but they were silent screams as her voice could not be heard. She kicked, pushed and made to run away from what she now realized was Karl's entity, but she realized that no matter how hard she tried, her legs were taking her nowhere. Cornered, she saw in horror Karl's entity raise a hack saw to cut off her head!

Rai suddenly woke up from the long horrific nightmare, her face ashen, to find Marie standing by her bedside.

"What's the matter with you? Why are you awake at this time? Are you a night hawk?" Marie asked.

Then Rai burst into tears.

"I've had a terrible nightmare about Karl's entity. It was about to cut my head off... in the same way he was killed," Rai replied, shaken to the core.

"An entity!" Marie said, her voice breaking in fear.

In fact, Rai had suspected something strange was going on in their town. She had heard different people relate their weird experiences but she pretended not to be afraid. After all she had just completed her karate lessons on self defense, and with the way she exercised every day she considered her self fit and capable of defending herself against any kind of furious attack.

That same night, there was another brilliant flash of lightening in another part of the town. When it lit up the sky Zwick, who had also been sleeping, woke up immediately. He found the house in complete darkness with just a splinter of little coming through the window, although he remembered leaving the lights on when he had gone to bed. Perhaps someone had turned them off as he was sleeping. Trying to imagine who it could be, he heard footsteps passing his door and then the door in the next room closing.

Wondering whether it was Mr. Dean moving through the house, he checked on him but was surprised to see Mr. Dean in a deep sleep in his bedroom. This puzzled Zwick. In fact, Zwick felt shaken at this, as he immediately guessed that it could be Karl's entity.

The next morning, in spite of their horrific experiences of the night before, Rai and Zwick were at the university attending lectures. So, too, were Marie and Matt.

"Rai, Rai," the lecturer called several times. "Are you here?"

Rai heard it as if the voice was coming from a long way off, but raised her hand. Then she noticed the other students, including Zwick, staring and smiling at her.

At the end of the lecture, she was asked to stay behind.

"Why do you look so worried? Be frank and tell us. It seems you have a big problem and that's not going to help you with your studies, so I think you need to relax," the lecturer said as Rai lowered her head. "You need to do something about it," he ordered her.

Loving and caring as Zwick was, he waited for her to emerge from the hall.

"Come on, what's your problem? Did anyone hurt you?" he asked her again and again as he took her hands in his.

"No," she said. "I'm just upset over the nightmare I had last night."

"You had one?" he asked, as held on to her hands and put his arms around her. "I had one as well."

"I have never suffered from such a nightmare before," Rai said.

And after she had told Zwick all about it he agonized about what they would have to do to annihilate Karl's entity as it had really started haunting as well as killing innocent people unreasonably, in every tragic way possible. He had heard that it always plucked out both the eyes and the heart of its victim, leaving scary holes in the bodies of the people it killed. Everyone who heard of it wondered how long it would be before it claimed a head.

CHAPTER ELEVEN

It was only a short time later that Mr. Dean was found dead in the most horrendous way. He had been found behind their house, hanging like a scare crow. His head had been cut off and was nowhere to be seen.

Although the sheriff hadn't truly believed Mr. Taji when he had visited him, the death of Mr. Dean made him have second thoughts about it and wondered if there was some truth to what Mr. Taji had said.

For the citizens however, there was no more wondering. This was final confirmation that Karl's entity was back and it had started with its evil deeds the same way his parents had done during their reign, although this one seemed more of revenge on a person who had stood witness to his execution.

A large number of people attended Mr. Dean's funeral, and Zwick was now more determined that ever to do what ever it took to prevent the entity from attacking the people further.

He did have his doubts, though, about stopping the entity since he no longer had the charmed necklace. He had given it to Whitney when they had still been friends. She had died without returning it and Zwick knew he may never get it back though it was vital to his life. He found it difficult to cope with the loss of his uncle and was often depressed.

Sometimes he even wondered if it was the absence of that necklace that had lead to the death of his uncle. He now blamed himself for not helping his uncle with his supernatural powers, but instead spending so much of his time with both Rai and Matt.

One afternoon, not very long after, Rai decided to go to the library after the day's lectures were over. While checking the book shelves, she came across a book that she had not noticed before, although she always visited the library regularly.

It looked interesting and appeared to be what she was looking for. Finding a seat in a corner she settled down to reading it. The book was about the supernatural and how to interpret supernatural occurrences. Having been written by a local writer she found references to Karl's family and their clandestine activities. She also read about how there was to be a bi centenary day when the souls of the dead people belonging to Karl's family would live again after the blood of any girl turning 20 on that day was spilt. It had been foretold that this would give them eternal evil powers. However, after they arose from the dead no human would live in Green Oasis town and there would only be the darkness of night over the town immediately after the eclipse.

Rai was so absorbed in the book that she did not notice Marie enter the library and she almost jumped out of her skin in fright when Marie spoke to her. But she returned the book to its shelf and left for the university once more with Marie where various co curricular activities were going on. Rai noticed that Matt was participating in an inter-house swimming event at the pool.

That night, after the lectures were over, the friends met up, but it had started showering outside. To the surprise of Rai and Marie, Zwick and Matt revealed that they were not going home but instead had decided to visit the old chateau that belonged to Karl's family because Zwick thought they could find something there which could help them to stop Karl's entity. The two of them had decided to enter the house on their own even though they knew that the police had cordoned off the house and they would be considered trespassers.

On reaching and entering the house they poked around for some time and then decided to go upstairs. There they found a room which was locked, but after a little tinkering around and a lot of pushing and kicking they managed to get the old door open. Switching on a light they found they were in some sort of storeroom in which family mementoes had been carelessly piled up. Glancing at different types of scary statues and albums, Zwick arrived at a photograph of Karl as a young lad and his mother when both were still alive. He immediately he decided to pocket it. In fact the walls were covered with pictures, many of them revealing that the family believed in evil and that sacrifices were a ritual to them.

A short time later, as they prepared to leave, Zwick telephoned Rai to remind her that she had to go with him to visit Madam Tabitha the next day.

That morning, as the sun rose in a clear blue sky, Zwick and Rai drove out to meet Madam Tabitha. They drove some kilometers without encountering any interference on the way.

Then Zwick stopped the car a few meters before the cave which was in the middle of the woodland.

"I just want you to stay right here in the car, and don't move," Zwick requested her.

"Yeah, I promise," she agreed locking the door. Then she settled back to wait. But a few minutes later she started looking around. The place looked strange to her as smoke filled the entrance of the cave and swirled out. She had heard of Madam Tabitha right from when she was young, but, although she didn't know her, she found the place to be creepy and frightening.

Later, amid the cries of different birds that filled the air she began hearing loud voices coming from the cave. Rai really had no idea why Zwick had decided to visit Madam Tabitha although she agreed to accompany him. However she was aware that people usually visited Madam Tabitha to find out something about Green Oasis seeing that she was the oldest living resident there. This didn't bother Rai as she remained waiting for Zwick. Then things got curious. There was a sudden silence as Zwick suddenly emerged from the smoke. In fact, Zwick had not really wanted to visit Madam Tabitha, but because that he knew that having lost his necklace his supernatural powers had been affected he had to consult her.

Zwick got into the car and drove off, but they had barely gone a short distance when his phone rang.

"What's up, Matt?" Zwick said, answering the call.

"Kent, who had just come out coma, has also been killed by the entity in the hospital, but this time the same doctor who was medicating Ms Darien had witnessed it. He also ran away to save himself, and no one tried to stop it as it raged about in the hospital," Matt said in the long telephone conversation.

"Oh God," Zwick said nervously.

"I'm so terrified of this ghost," Matt confessed.

Zwick did not bother to explain what had happened to Rai as she was quite timid and he did not want to scare her any more, frightened as she was by the nightmares she had had. Now that he knew that the entity had killed Kent, Zwick realized it was their turn to watch out. He knew they had to find some way of protecting themselves before they could be attacked.

Later Zwick told her that Madam Tabitha had told him that the culprit was growing stronger each and every day that passed by.

"It will kill us all," Rai commented, her voice suddenly cracking with fear.

Zwick had to meet Matt at the campus, because it was the day of the swimming event finals and Matt was among the finalists.

Sitting comfortably watching the contest from chairs at the pool side, they both wished Matt would emerge winner, in first place.

Matt was soon in the lead with four points, but as soon as they blew the whistle for the last round, Zwick started feeling uncomfortable. Although nothing appeared to be wrong with the place at that moment, the lights started dazzling his eyes. His highly tuned instinct told him something strange was about to happen at any moment.

Suddenly as the place was crowded with different students; the entity emerged from the pool waters, near the finishing line. Those who saw it observed that it had no head, and they all took off, as fast as they could, fearing for their lives. There was mayhem as students pushed past each other all in a terrible hurry trying to exit from the pool side at breakneck speed. However the entity finally disappeared without hurting any student.

Later in the evening, Zwick went with Rai to the hostel to meet Marie and take her with them to the Hard Rock Pub to refresh themselves and hopefully get over the events of the day at the campus.

As they opened the door to the apartment they found Marie busy organizing her books in a bag. She was not willing to go with them to the pub, but Zwick and Rai sat around hoping they could convince her to go with them once she had finished packing. It was quite by chance that Zwick, with his sharp eyes, noticed a necklace in Marie's bag. It looked very familiar. In fact it looked vary much like the one he had given to Whitney. He was not sure it was, but he just had to know.

"Marie, where did you get that necklace?" Zwick asked her.

"I don't really know. I found it when cleaning up the place after my birthday celebrations. Although I've tried to find the owner I've been unsuccessful so far," Marie replied.

Zwick explained to Marie that it was his and was extremely relieved when Marie returned it to him. He was afraid it had been lost to him forever since he had not been in contact with Whitney for some time prior to her death. He thanked Marie for it and left with Rai a short time later.

But she was not alone for very long because there was a knock on the door and Matt came in, looking very unhappy.

"What's wrong Matt? Are you okay?" Marie asked him, her concern showing in her voice.

"Of course not," Matt replied.

"I know you cheated on me. I saw you at the swimming contest before the entity chase," Matt exclaimed hotly.

"What the hell are you talking about? Is that why you're here?" Marie asked him.

She was upset at his allegations.

"I think you know whom, when, where and why. I'm not a kid," Matt said seriously.

"If you're going to talk like that I would like you to leave," Marie demanded her voice tremulous.

"Fine, I wish you all the best," Matt said as he banged the door and left, leaving Marie to collapse in a flood of tears.

Marie, though, was more puzzled than upset. She just couldn't figure out what Matt was talking about. She knew she had given no reason to Matt to believe she was cheating on him.

She spent the rest of the evening cleaning up the room, keeping herself busy, doing anything to get her mind off Matt and his accusations.

Later that night Zwick and Rai returned cruising up to the main gate of their hostel.

As Rai turned to enter the door Zwick held her hand back. He looked at her dearly and would have loved to hold her tenderly but he had to let her go.

"Marie? What's wrong? Why are you crying?" Rai asked her friend as she entered and saw her friend's tear stained face.

"I know breaking up is hard but I don't want ever to see Matt again," Marie said, her head bowed and in tears.

"Did you fight with him?" Rai asked worriedly.

"No, but he accused me of things I haven't done. And he's so jealous of my friends," she said angrily.

But not only was she angry with Matt. She now

worried that the rumors that she was dating other guys would be flying thick and fast all over the University.

"Love is something grand. Don't lose that feeling. I know how it hurts but just try to forget that anything happened between you and him," Rai told Marie, by way of advice.

Sometime later Marie settled down and tried to get her mind on other things. Then her phone started demanding her attention, ringing shrilly and incessantly. Looking at it she noticed that it was Matt who was phoning but she didn't really want to talk to him just then so she did not reply. Suddenly it stopped and all was quiet in the room once more.

"Marie, get serious, why didn't you pick up the phone?" Rai asked her awkwardly.

"I just need more time alone," Marie explained. "Besides, I want to get some sleep, now," she continued as she turned the lights out.

Finally, after much tossing and turning and a whole lot of heart searching, Marie drifted off into a fitful sleep.

Then, at around 3:30am, Marie and Rai really were finally sleeping soundly when a storm picked up. The wind blew strongly and flashes of lightning streaked across the sky followed by loud clashes of thunder. Both the girls were so exhausted by the turn of events that day that they were undisturbed by it, however, and slept right through it.

Neither did they notice the shapeless form that crept into the room and made its way first to Rai's bed and then to Marie's. They were still too fast asleep to notice it yet.

It was only when Marie turned that she noticed that her blanket had fallen off. She reached for it to cover herself but it seemed to be stuck on something.

Opening her eyes to see what had caught her blanket, she became aware of a foul smell assailing her nostrils. It was the stench of rotten meat.

Marie looked across the room at the clock on the other wall. But she was immediately transfixed with fear for where the clock should have been she noticed a vague indefinable moving slowly towards her. Instinctively she knew it had to be Karl's ghost.

She opened her mouth to scream but no sound came from it. She hoped Rai would hear her and come to her aid, but Rai slept on as though she couldn't hear anything, in fact, as if she was dead.

Marie kept screaming, "Rai, help, meeeeeeee." But Rai slept on as if she was unable to hear anything of what was going on in the room.

Finally, after what seemed an eternity to Marie, although it had really been a few moments, the ghost threw Marie to the floor with a mocking smile and then started jabbing her in the chest with its claw like fingers getting at her heart.

Then, in a matter of a moment, it lifted Marie up and hung her from the ceiling fan.

Rai didn't budge an inch. How was she to know her friend was now dead?

Matt, meanwhile, had had a sleepless night too, and by the first hint of the next morning he had come to a decision. He would go to the hostel at the earliest and apologize to Marie for the way he had behaved the previous night.

All was still quiet at the hostel when Matt arrived. The hostel was as quiet as ever, and he continued through the silent corridor. He walked up to Marie's room and almost stepped into a pool of blood oozing from the under the door. Rushing to the door and banging on it with his fists, he called out to Marie. After a few minutes when nobody responded, he kicked the door open with all his strength, and entered.

"Oh no," Matt heard himself cry.

It was unbelievable. Matt couldn't take his eyes off Marie hanging from the ceiling fan, dead, with a deep hole between her breasts, and her eyes gouged out.

It was only then that Rai awoke groggily. She became conscious of someone crying loudly but thought the sound must be coming from somewhere else in the hostel, unaware it was happening in her own room. Like a swimmer trying to rise to the surface of the water, she struggled awake, opened her eyes and was surprised to find Matt inside the room. She wondered how Matt had entered their room and why he was crying. Then she saw Marie, and passed out in sheer shock.

By now others had noticed the commotion and an ambulance had been summoned. Rai was sedated and carried away on a stretcher.

The news of Marie's death spread like wildfire all over the campus and then all over Green Oasis. Matt himself felt as if he was going crazy, and despite the sheriff's reassuring messages to the people of Green Oasis town, the death of Marie revealed more than ever the helplessness of the concerned authorities in protecting the people from Karl's entity.

CHAPTER TWELVE

Time, as it will, passed however, and it was about six months later that some semblance of normalcy returned to the town. People were going about their business as usual, students were attending the university one more and young couples were dating all over again.

Zwick returned to Madam Tabitha for answers and for advice. She explained to him how Karl's entity was able to do what it did- the power lay in the bangle. According to her, this bangle had existed for over four centuries and it had remained in the possession of one family.

Madam Tabitha also explained to Zwick that he, too, could use his supernatural powers because he possessed the magical necklace that she had given him.

Taken aback, and rubbing his lower lip with the necklace he asked her, "How did you know, Madam Tabitha?"

"What do you mean?" she asked Zwick. "Of course I know about it. In fact it once belonged to me. It's quite along story, but when I was just about a month old I was diagnosed with a hard to treat disease. My parents took me to the place of a woman to be looked after. They knew she had special powers, and she would help me survive. Because she was barren I became the child she could never have and she took me to her heart.

When I was eventually cured of my disease she gave me this necklace. My parents never came back for me although after some time my uncle did eventually. I had the necklace with me for many years, until I passed it onto someone needier than me   but I have followed its movements and am well aware that it is in your possession, Zwick," he said.

Zwick returned home and after sun down, he went to bed. Because of his trip to Madam Tabitha he hadn't met up with Rai that day which was quite unusual, for Rai was now the first thing on his mind when he awoke and the last thing on his mind when he went to sleep. It was to be Rai's twenty second birthday the next day, and promising himself he would make it a memorable one, he fell asleep.

A short time later he started dreaming. To his horror it was about Rai being captured by Karl's entity and taken to an old chateau where it had made preparations to sacrifice her, it coincidentally being a memorial day for its ancestors. Unfortunately he was too late to save her. Finding her lifeless body he dropped to the knees and cradled her head in his arms. Karl, in the meantime, having gained full strength of his powers, suddenly appeared. Then his ancestors started emerging from out of nowhere, and commanded Karl to kill Zwick.

But as the entity raised the axe to cut off his head Zwick suddenly awoke from the horrible nightmare in a cold sweat.

Taking time to analyze his terrible dream, he knew that Rai was the next target for this entity and that's why it did not kill her in the hostel when it killed Marie, because she was to be sacrificed in a special way on a special day.

Determined to protect Rai from the entity and certain death, he picked her up early next morning and took her to Madam Tabitha's place, to inform her about his nightmare and to seek her help.

"But why did she decide to live alone in the woodlands all by herself?" Rai

asked Zwick as they were racing through the woodlands.

"Well, since her parents deserted her she never wanted to live with people again after her guardian died and so she found this lonely shelter in the woodlands," Zwick replied, noting that they weren't very far off by then.

Tyres screamed and brakes screeched as they came to a sudden halt outside the cave. Zwick lit a candle he had brought with him and they entered the dark and foreboding place.

Rai was on edge and started looking around but she could see nothing because the place was full of thick mist, the source of which she could not discover. Sensing her discomfort Zwick took her by the hand and led her deep down into the entrails of the cave.

Finally they discerned a ray of light and walked toward it.

"She is my friend," Zwick replied in a loud voice to the query that was thrust upon them as soon as they entered the small circle of light.

Rai remained silent and remained so all the time while Zwick narrated all the events of the past few days to his silent and invisible listener. Although Zwick knew he was talking to Madam Tabitha, Rai believed the deep voice that had spoken to them belonged to a man.

"Now son," the voice boomed, "the powers you have cannot defeat that entity because it uses the powers of the souls of people it kills in addition, so it's much stronger than you are. But if tomorrow there is no lunar eclipse to make you powerful and strong enough, your lovely friend is going to be sacrificed no matter what. If you try to stop it without your immortal powers you, too, will be killed. However there will be no more day time in Green Oasis town. We shall be experiencing nights only after the entity sacrifices her."

In the silence that followed this revelation, Zwick thought about how, if the eclipse didn't occur, he would not be able to save Rai, although he was feeling capable of doing anything with the few abilities he had just then. But he believed Madam Tabitha's advice as the last resort to help him solve his problems.

"Then how will I know that it is eclipse time?" Zwick asked Madam Tabitha.

"My son, believe in your powers. You will know that automatically, but it will happen at 10:00 pm, and, son, after you receive the power to save the town and your friend, you will never see me again," Madam Tabitha said in a strong echoing voice.

Later, after getting all the information he needed, he and Rai waved goodbye to Madam Tabitha, and left the woodland as early as they could for it was getting late.

"Why doesn't she reveal her face?" Rai asked Zwick.

"No one has ever seen her face apart from her parents because she was born misshapen and she is completely bald," he said to her.

For the next few days the air was hazy in Green Oasis town which was quite normal for that time of the year, but Zwick was on edge and more so the day he and Rai had to go earlier to the campus on the second anniversary of that terrible day at the University.

It was during the memorial ceremony that he told Rai that something was wrong at the farm. He wanted to go there immediately to check something out immediately. He had just received an anonymous call that someone was busy riding horses all over the paddock. He worried about things on his way to the paddock. He wondered if it was the entity playing games with him, although he was not afraid to face it, however ugly things might turn out to be.

He returned to the ceremony some time later, at exactly 9:00pm. Both Rai and Matt had grown worried already thinking that he may have met with some problems on the way although they knew he was a super hero, always ready for a challenge under any kind of circumstance.

Surprisingly, he had found all the horses grazing as usual and no one was there on the farm which left him puzzled for a while because the woman's voice at the other end had seemed so definite about what was going on.

Looking up at the sky, he thought he was seeing the first signs of the eclipse as the night became darker than usual.

But while Rai was chatting with the other students Zwick requested Matt to take care of her as he was expecting something to happen at any time. From there he went to the library to check out the ancient book Rai had told him about.

After some time, Matt glanced at where Rai had been standing with some other girls, and she was not there. When he asked the girls where she had gone, they said she was in the pantry room. Unfortunately after waiting for more than twenty minutes, they wondered if Rai had been taken away by the entity.

Matt, feeling very worried as he didn't know where to start, informed Zwick about it.

"Zwick, Rai is gone. It has just taken her now," Matt said nervously.

Utterly taken aback, Zwick was in a dilemma. because he knew if he got all his powers, he was not going to ever see Madam Tabitha again, and if the eclipses failed, he was going to die trying to rescue Rai from the ghostly old chateau. But there were only fifteen minutes left for the full moon eclipse to take place, so Zwick decided to run like the wind up to the chateau where he suspected Rai had been taken.

Eventually, he arrived at the house which was completely hidden by overgrown bushes as it was no longer lived in by the family to which it had belonged. But as he entered through the first door, it swung shut behind him. Looking back he saw that nobody had shut it but he did not think too much about it as there were some winds blowing.

He checked the house room by room, floor by floor, all the while calling out to Rai. Then, finally, walking down the narrow corridor at the rear of the second floor, he saw Rai unconscious and spread-eagled on a sack, ready to be sacrificed. Heart thudding, he raced to Rai. A vague form, which, all too late, he realized was the entity, prevented him from approaching her and started attacking him vigorously. It was as if it knew that Zwick would be the spoke in the wheel and would deter him from his mission with the few powers he had.

Zwick and the entity wrestled. After a few minutes of wrestling, Zwick tried to regain his breath. Suddenly the entity again grabbed him and threw him downstairs. But Zwick held on to it and they both went crashing down into a pile of timber below. The entity came out of it instantly since it was more powerful than Zwick. Seeing him weakened, it went back upstairs to where Rai was, to continue with its sacrifice.

Zwick started to pull himself out of the timber pile he had fallen into. Lying on his back, looking up at the sky, he remembered Madam Tabitha's last words to him. It was then that he realized then there were only a few moments before the eclipse would take place and he had to do something or all would be lost.

It was also at that very same moment that something extraordinary occurred.

As clouds raced across the sky and darkened it for a moment, red rays appeared out of nowhere and struck straight Zwicks' bare chest, striking the necklace around his neck, filling the beads with a fiery red light. All this took but a few moments and Zwick was barely conscious as the process was taking place.

Now Matt who had guessed where Zwick was going and had followed him to the chateau was in the near by bushes and had watched the battle dumbfounded. He saw the entity now moving towards Zwick with an axe preparing to behead him exactly as it intended to before it sacrificed Rai. Unfortunately he was too mesmerized by this sudden and violent turn of events to do anything to save Zwick besides which he realized that Zwick was also a superhuman, and what he had witnessed had been a battle between two super humans.

"Am I watching a movie scene or is it for real?" he questioned himself as he rubbed the palm of his hand over his eyes.

He was still rooted to the spot, incapable of moving a muscle as he watched the entity move up behind Zwick a few moments later, and raise the axe to behead him.

Fortunately Zwick seemed to have regained his consciousness and his super natural strength. He reached out and grabbed hold of the blade. From his hiding place, Matt winced, convinced that Zwick would have cut his hand in the process.

But foreboding turned to an incredulous surprise and relief as he watched Zwick snap the blade as one would a twig in the palm of his hand and scatter the broken pieces before the entity in contempt.

By now Zwick had grown so powerful that his eyes, too, glowed red as he fought the entity as he had never fought before.

Finally the entity disappeared from the scene of the epic battle. Surprisingly, with all his natural powers it was helpless in the face of Zwicks' new found power and his dogged determination to rid Green Oasis once and for all of the menace.

With these new powers Zwick could now discover the entity no matter where it tried to hide from him. It, by then, had begun to realize that Zwick was of superior strength and recognizing that it was getting weak, decided to avoid any further conflict, but rather complete the job it had originally set out to do- sacrifice Rai.

The long struggle, the falls it had taken and the injuries it incurred had all weakened the entity, particularly as it had taken the human form of Mr. Dean and could therefore feel the pain of a human body grievously injured.

Matt, in the meantime, had collected his wits about him and emerged from his hiding place to assist Zwick.

Seeing him, Zwick called out loudly, "Matt move inside and release Rai from the cross."

Matt, still feeling threatened by the entity looked across at it for a moment. Then, seeing it was enmeshed in a tangle of wires and was busy trying to extinguish the flames in which it was engulfed, he went to Rai, freed her and carried her out gently. By then Zwick had choked the entity with wires and fire, until he was definitely sure that it had died for the second time.

Then Zwick pushed the metal plate on which the entity was up to the place where the blaze was now strongest. Then there was a stunned silence, before Zwick spoke to Karl's ghost.

"You have taken the souls people of many people that we loved and who were important to us. They were innocent and did not deserve to die the way they did. So now I'm sending you to hell for real."

The blaze spread further all over the body of Mr. Dean and the piteous cries of numerous souls filled the air and persisted until the body was finally reduced to ashes.

Zwick held Rai in his arms, and crooned comfortingly until she regained consciousness some time later. When she did, the first thing she saw was Zwicks' face. They hugged and murmured sweet nothings between sobs of relief until finally, exhausted, they drifted off into a relieved silence.

A year passed and people had once again started living with no fear of the entity in Green Oasis. Zwick himself had started living a happy life after saving Rai because she was now completely his and they concentrated on their studies as they had previously. Zwick was now a local hero for bringing some semblance of normalcy to the town.

Karl's family property was converted into a park which became very popular with the people of Green Oasis who collected there regularly to have fun. Life at the university had returned to normal as well.

As graduation day neared it was decided to hold the ceremony in the new park. There would be enough space to accommodate all the guests who had been invited to the ceremony.

This was a happy time for all the well wishers of Green Oasis University. Putting all the tragedy behind, Zwick, Rai and the other graduates looked radiant in their blue graduation gowns. Just a short while ago both Zwick and Rai had never thought they would be celebrating this day because of the mayhem the entity was causing. But now it had been destroyed and it was time to put those bad times behind them. This was the day to rejoice with friends, families and fellow students who never gave up their studies even as the entity claimed the lives of their loved ones.

At the ceremony, Zwick and Rai sat comfortably in the back row. Behind them were some young kids playing football. Soon it would be time for Rai and Zwick and all the other graduates to collect their certificates.

Then Zwicks' name was called out. As he walked up to the dais he left Rai sitting with some other students in the same row with them.

Rai glanced for a moment at the boys who were playing and noticed that one of them had kicked the ball a distance. She didn't think too much of it as the boys ran to pick up their ball and one of them approached the park fence.

Following the ball, the boy bent to pick it up and that was when he noticed something half buried in the dirt. He ignored his ball and instead pulled the object out of the soil, examining it closely.

He looked at it and recognized it as being some sort of ornament but wasn't to know that it was the bangle that had supposedly been destroyed along with Karl's ghost in the inferno.

This was definitely bad news. The bangle was not something to be treated lightly, associated as it was with demons and black evil powers from the oceans and seas. Now, despite the fact that the people of Green Oasis had tried to get rid of this evil bangle for centuries, it looked as if they never could. It seemed immortal. Now, having been deprived of Karl, it was readying to prey upon the young boy.

Pocketing the bangle, the innocent boy started walking slowly back to where he had been playing football with his friends. However, his eyes were now pools of empty blackness and an indefinable iciness coursed through his veins.

CHAPTER THIRTEEN

Two months later, on a sunny morning, Zwick woke from a deep and satisfying sleep. Life was looking up once more for him. He had put the past behind him, immersed himself in his studies, and held on to his job at the paddock.

At around 9:00am that morning, he drove off as usual to the paddock in his Chevrolet pickup. Then, work completed, he drove back through the streets of Green Oasis. Suddenly he hit the brakes.

"Hey, Matt," he called out to his friend whom he spotted across the street. "Let's ride out to the park."

"Hey, how could you be here, man?" Matt asked him incredibly as they drove off.

"As you know, I had to go to the farm before I came to town," Zwick said. In the park Matt and Zwick found Rai waiting for them and he sat down on the bench beside them, placing his cap on his lap.

"I didn't expect to find so many people here at this time," said Matt.

"You guys, I have been waiting for quite a while. What took you so long?" Rai asked Zwick and Matt.

"Nothing much. We just hung out on the way, but at least we're here," replied Matt smiling.

"By the way, what do you Rai say to joining us on a small holiday trip tomorrow?" asked Zwick.

"Where?" Rai asked, anxious to know.

"The Dead Sea Beach. Remember that resort?" replied Zwick.

"Well, I'll try to make it," Rai said with a quick smile.

Later, after dropping Matt off, Zwick entered the local store.

"Can we have some salmon sandwiches?" Zwick asked as Rai stood beside him.

"Of course, you can," the elderly supermarket attendant replied but surprisingly kept staring at the young couple as if she had seen them somewhere before.

The scrutiny made Rai feel uncomfortable as she picked up the parcel.

"Oh, pretty heavy," she remarked as she made for the door.

Zwick, too, was uncomfortable at the attendant's scrutiny, but didn't worry about it for too long.

Back home, Rai immediately started packing her bag for the trip next day.

She thought about how she had missed the previous trip when Karl had taken the group there. She hoped she would enjoy herself with Zwick and Matt there.

The next morning the four met up and boarded the boat along with a number of other people who seemed to be on their way to the Dead Sea Resort, too. As the boat started sailing, memories of the first trip flashed through Zwicks' mind. But the journey took a little less than an hour and they reached the resort before the sun was too hot.

"Come on guys, and experience nature," Matt yelled at Zwick and Rai as they were alighting. Zwick looked around and was quite surprised to note that the beach looked more attractive this time than it had when he had been there before with Whitney.

Rai, however, was not too enamored by the place at first. She did not care too much for sand and prickly bushes. She wondered why Zwick loved this place so much. But when she noticed the butterflies and different species of birds, some of which she had never seen before, she understood its charm.

At sunset she was amazed at the thousands of white bats that fluttered by. Suddenly she was cold. Why did they remind her of that awful night at the university when hundreds of students rushed helter skelter, running away from trouble?

By about 7:00 that evening the only light on the beach came from a ghostly moon covered by dark clouds, and the fire they had lit on the beach. They then decided to call it a day and camp on the beach for the night.

Inside their tent, Zwick kissed Rai on the check as he helped her to zip herself into her sleeping bag. She smiled as she slumbered innocently besides him.

She was awoken some hours later by the warmth of the sun on her face. "Wow, is it morning?" Rai asked stretching slowly and languidly.

"Yeah. How did you sleep? I hardly slept at all," replied Matt getting out of his bag.

As they readied themselves for the day Matt stepped out of the tent and made for some bushes to answer nature's call. Standing beneath a tree and looking up, he heard a sudden sound in the bushes before him. Peering through the leaves he saw a young kid, about 3ft tall and very frail, standing in front of him. Taken off guard and in a state of shock, Matt took off without once looking back.

Zwick and Rai saw him running at breakneck speed toward them and wondered what it was all about.

When he told them about the kid they thought his imagination had got the better of him.

"I think you just saw a scarecrow and then you decided to run. Common sense will tell you you can't find a kid in a bush in the middle of nowhere," Zwick said, showing Matt that nobody believed him."

Matt knew it would be hopeless trying to convince them of what he had seen and let it go at that.

Rai and Zwick started moving out. Matt somehow felt terrified about what he had seen although his friends had not believed him. But as he had no other alternative except to stay on and encounter the child once again, he decided to follow them.

Printed in the United Kingdom by
Lightning Source UK Ltd., Milton Keynes
136909UK00001B/289/P